I Can Make You Love Me

NADIA NICOLE

MAJOR KEY
PUBLISHING

This book is dedicated to everyone who believes in true love.... You know the love that you can't go a day without. The love that radiates from your heart and pierces your soul. Relish in the moments that take your breath away and cherish the people who love you unconditionally.

Synopsis

Grieving the loss of her mother, Sundai returns home to plan a funeral and finds solace in the unlikeliest of places—Bryce, her mother's neighbor. As they navigate the delicate dance of grief and unexpected connection, Sundai grapples with guilt for falling for Bryce during such a somber time. To complicate matters, Bryce's Brother, Lucas, starts spreading vicious rumors about Sundai, fueled by jealousy. His motives are confirmed to be the product of his desire for her. Faced with the turmoil of emotions and the hurtful rumors, Sundai decides to distance herself and returns home.

Bryce can't shake the profound impact Sundai has had on him. Unable to get her off his mind, he's driven to take a leap of faith and flies halfway across the country to find her. I Can Make You Love Me weaves a tale of love emerging from the depths of grief, exploring the complexities of guilt, jealousy, and the resilience of the human heart. Will Sundai and Bryce overcome the obstacles and find a way to heal together, or will the challenges they face prove insurmountable in the pursuit of love and happiness?

CHAPTER 1

Sundai

The phone rang with news that caused my knees to buckle under me. My already swollen and inflamed knee came crashing into the hardwood floor of my apartment. Pain radiated its way from my heart, disguising the pain that I should've felt in my knee.

"Hello?" the voice called over the phone.

I couldn't respond. Tears choked any sound that I could've produced. I felt like I was drowning in my own tears, and there was no one there to save me. I instantly regretted every decision I had made over the past nine months. I hated the fact that I chose to move halfway across the country to chase my dream as a broadcast journalist. I should've stayed in Alabama with my mother. I should have chosen family over everything, and I definitely should have returned home when her home health nurse called and said that her health was failing. My mother rebuked the idea with everything in her, and she insisted that I stay put.

I had just started my internship and missing any days would have hindered me tremendously. She understood that and insisted that I didn't come home. I heeded her advice and stayed in New York City.

"Sundai, are you there," Constance called over the phone.

Constance had been my mother's nurse for months, and I anticipated her daily phone call with updates on my mother's condition. I never expected that this phone call would come early, and it would be the phone call that changed my life forever.

"I'm here," I finally managed to speak despite the snot that was running down my nose.

I was sitting in the middle of the floor struggling to hold the phone up to my ear, but I wanted to hear what Constance was saying. A part of me wanted her to tell me that it was an April Fool's joke. We were a little way past April—four months to be exact. So, I knew the punchline wasn't coming.

"I'm sorry," she said, "I got here this morning, and she was unconscious on the living room floor."

"But, how? I thought she was progressing."

My mother had been diagnosed with breast cancer, but she was doing chemo regularly. She had her good days and her bad ones. I just didn't understand how things could go south so quickly.

"I have no answer for that, but she's not suffering anymore," she spoke the last line as if it were supposed to bring some sort of comfort. It did not.

She may not have been suffering anymore, but I knew that it was only the beginning of my suffering. I wrestled with the thought of living the rest of my life without my mother. It wasn't something I wanted to think about at that moment.

"I'll be there as soon as I can," I told her before disconnecting the call.

I sat in the middle of the floor and let the grief overcome me. I wept out loud for hours. I cried until I didn't have another tear to cry. No one could understand the pain that I felt. Death is one thing, but losing your mother was indescribable. I was an only child, and my father wasn't around so naturally, I clung to Opal. She was my lifeline, and I wasn't sure what I was going to do without her. The first thing I had to do was make arrangements to go back to Alabama.

I hadn't been back since I left, and now I had to plan a

funeral. I wasn't feeling it at all, but I went to my laptop and sent my boss an e-mail to let her know that I was leaving town, and I didn't know for how long. I checked on and purchased a plane ticket for the next day before I packed a bag. I sucked up my feelings and climbed into bed. The next day was going to be the start of several long days, and I needed as much rest as I could get.

CHAPTER 2

Bryce

The day was long, and I was glad to hear the final bell ringing. Working with kids was not for the faint of heart, especially disorderly high school children who landed their way in summer school. I took the job as physical education teacher and head football coach of the Cooperville Mavericks in hopes of changing somebody's child's life. Today though, they had me bent out of shape and I was ready to kick off my shoes and relax. I couldn't wait to get to my quiet three-bedroom stucco and prop my feet up. Anyone who said aging was a graceful process lied. My knees popped all day, and I only found relief when I was off my feet.

I turned into the neighborhood, and all happiness was absorbed from my body when I saw the plethora of cars that were gathered at Mrs. Opal's house. She was elderly, and I knew that she was sickly. However, she hadn't lost an ounce of spunk. Seeing her was the highlight of my day. She reminded me of my grand-mother, Geraldine, who died when I was younger. I didn't have many memories with Geraldine, but in the short time that I moved to Cooperville I had created plenty of memories with Opal. I sat in my driveway and recalled the moment I first met her.

I had only been in Cooperville for a week. I didn't know anyone, but I hadn't really made it my business to reach out and be neigh-borly either. I was a creature of habit, and I preferred to stay to myself. It was early one Saturday morning, and I sat on my patio sipping Folgers with French vanilla creamer. It was my morning routine. I would enjoy the fresh air, birds chirping, and my daily dose of caffeine. There was nothing like fresh air in the morning time before the obligations of the day took over. I sipped from my coffee mug as I watched a fawn emerge from the wood line. We were in rural Alabama, so seeing a deer here and there wasn't a surprise. I sat motionless as I observed the baby that wobbled from the woods and directly into my neighbor's garden. It snatched a tomato from its vine before I felt compelled to shoo it away. I thought momen-tarily about my next move. The neighbor had several ripe tomatoes that needed to be plucked. I knew that she was elderly, and I had never seen anyone else living there with her. The thought came instantaneously as I rose from my chair and grabbed a plastic bowl from my kitchen. I waltzed right down the stairs of my patio and into her small garden. I moved with skilled precision so as to not disturb the cabbage or other vegetables that she had planted. I plucked a couple of tomatoes before I heard her screen door squeak open.

"Son, I know you aren't over here stealing," a little brown skinned woman with curly silvering hair said to me as soon as her feet hit the ground, "a lot of blood, sweat, and tears went into those 'maters."

"No ma'am," I replied, "You had a deer in your garden, and I saw that these were ripe, so I plucked them for you."

I handed her the plastic bowl as a smile spread across her face. The previous hostility melted away. She took the bowl but eyed me up and down before she spoke again.

"What do you know about gardening?" she asked, "I see you out here every morning sipping coffee like the city folks."

I couldn't help but laugh as I imagined her little nosey self peeking out her window every morning watching me. She reminded me of my grandmother so much that it wasn't funny. Geraldine didn't care what came out of her mouth.

5

"I was raised by my grandmother, Geraldine, and she had a garden too, I informed her.

"Well, I was wondering when you were going to come over and introduce yourself," she said, "I'm Opal."

"Bryce," I said as I extended my hand to shake hers.

"Bryce, honey, grab one of those green maters off the vine, and come inside," she instructed, "I'll fry it for us."

I wasn't prepared to turn down a fried green tomato, nor was I prepared to tussle with the little old lady that was eyeing me down from her backdoor. She seemed like she was a force to be reckoned with, and I had better sense than to get on her bad side. I grabbed the green tomato like she told me and proceeded inside of her home. A bull mastiff puppy greeted me. Even though his face was young, his body was huge, and he was baring his teeth. It was clear that he was protective of Ms. Opal, and I was the stranger in his home. I froze in my tracks and could literally hear my heart thumping in my ear.

"Don't mind him," Opal spoke, "Kane's just a big baby."

"Come on here and leave our neighbor alone," she said, directing that statement at the dog, "he didn't steal my maters."

Almost as if she spoke a language that he understood, he turned and followed her into the kitchen. I chuckled slightly at the "mater" comment. I felt like I wasn't going to live that down as long as I lived next to Opal and Kane. She went about her business slicing and frying tomatoes from her garden. I sat at the kitchen table and watched her intently as made small talk. That was my first of many encounters when it came to Opal Johnson.

I sat in the driveway as I reminisced about the times I had with Mrs. Opal. I was always there to do odd and end jobs for her when needed, and she would cook Sunday dinner and invite me over. She would always tell me about her daughter that moved to New York to pursue her dreams, and I would see pictures of her hanging around the house. She was breathtaking to say the least, and I would always tell Opal that I would watch whatever new station she ended up on.

I composed my thoughts and climbed out of my Jeep

Compass. I placed my briefcase on the hood of the car and walked towards Mrs. Opal's front door. Kane came barreling from down the street towards me as I approached his house. He was frantic and disoriented. Mrs. Opal didn't let him outside alone, so I knew that something was awry. I grabbed him by the collar and drug him towards the front door. I was met at the door by Mrs. Opal's nurse.

"There you are!" She exclaimed as she saw me with the dog, "He bolted out of the door when the ambulance came. I think the siren startled him.

"Ambulance?" The pit in my stomach grew. I felt like something was wrong, and the more she spoke the more she solidified my hunch.

"Yes. Opal went on to glory sometime during the night. It's protocol for me to call the ambulance, but she was gone."

Her eyes glossed with tears, and I could tell that she had grown somewhat attached to Opal—as had I. It was hard not to. She had an infectious personality that reminded me of the corner piece of a brownie. It was a tad bit crunchy around the edges, but it was soft and gooey once you got to know her. Silence interrupted the space between us as we searched for words to say. Kane started barking at something in the distance. He jumped up and attempted to take off, but I yanked him back by his collar. He jerked back to his original position and sat looking at me as if he wanted to speak words but couldn't. I felt bad for choking him out, but the last thing we needed was a hundred-pound mastiff terrorizing the neighborhood.

"That dog is terrible," she said to me, "Opal had him spoiled rotten. I don't what he's going to do tonight."

"Tonight?"

"Yes. Sundai will be here sometime tomorrow," she explained, "Have you met her yet?"

I shook my head. Opal and I had only spoken about the elusive Sundai. I never had the privilege of meeting her face to face. Even though her mother just passed, a part of me was excited to have the opportunity.

"I'll keep the dog tonight and return him when Sundai arrives tomorrow," I suggested.

Constance nodded her head, expression full of relief. I could tell that her and Kane weren't the best of friends, and it tickled me. She disappeared into the house and returned with a bag of pedigree dry dog food.

"Have fun," she said sarcastically.

I drug Kane across Opal's lawn and mine and into my house. I was hesitant to take the leash off him, but I knew that he couldn't stay attached to it all night. He sniffed around my house until he found a cozy spot in the living room to lie down. I felt like he had an eventful afternoon, so I let him be.

I can't wait to see what tomorrow holds for both of us," I thought to myself.

CHAPTER 3
Sundai

I pulled my luggage through John F. Kennedy International Airport. It was jam-packed with travelers as usual, and I didn't like it one bit. My rolling suitcase seemed heavier than usual. I instantly regretted packing so much. I should have packed the bare minimum and bought anything else when I got back to Alabama. Attitude set in as I checked in. The flight attendant took my bag and informed me that the plane wasn't boarding right away.

"It should be another thirty minutes or so," she informed me, "we will announce when your flight is boarding over the loudspeaker."

I nodded my head in understanding. I knew that I had arrived a little early, but the last thing I wanted to do was stand in line with the rest of the last-minute travelers. Arriving early allowed me to breathe easier as I made my way over to the Dunkin' Donuts that I passed on the way to the check-in counter. I perused the menu momentarily before I noticed a pair of eyes staring at me from across the lobby. He was seated with a laptop open on his lap, but his attention was not focused on the screen at all. His eyes met mine, and I smiled sheepishly. His rich chocolate skin and neatly trimmed beard and goatee gave him a professional vibe.

"May I take your order?" a young twenty-something woman asked as the person in front of me retrieved their order and left.

I turned my attention from the handsome stranger and back to the counter ahead of me.

"Yea. Can I get a medium Caramel Craze iced latte?"

"Whole milk or skim milk?"

"Whole please," I responded as I pulled out my debit card to pay for the drink.

Moments later, I found myself sipping my latte sitting in the same lobby as the man that was previously staring me down from across the airport. I sat a few rows in front of him, but my seat faced his and I could see him clearly. I took a few sips of my drink as his eyes darted from the computer screen to me. He was trying his hardest to be inconspicuous, and I found it comical. Time ticked by as we played a sort of cat and mouse game. I would gaze around the airport people watching, but my gaze would always find his again. He typed away on his laptop, but I could tell that I was easily distracting him. Our awkward misery ended when they called my gate over the loudspeaker.

I jumped up and trudged towards the appropriate gate. Every step was a step closer to the reality of what was waiting for me in Alabama when I got there. I never thought I would be burying my mother as soon as I was. We had plenty of talks about her passing away. She accepted her diagnosis, and she understood that she had to leave this world one day. I refused to accept it; however. She was my mother, and in my eyes, she was a superwoman. I thought surely, she would beat this like she beat everything else. She survived a difficult labor with me. The doctors were preparing for the "save your baby or save yourself" speech, but Opal wasn't hearing it. She advocated for herself and for me, and we both made it through. She made it through an abusive relationship with my father, Franklin. She had been through so much, but apparently breast cancer was her Achilles heel.

I was so absorbed in my own thoughts that I didn't notice the handsome man close his laptop, rise from his chair, or saunter towards the same gate that I was walking through. We were halfway through the jet bridge before his cologne caught my attention. It was swirling in the enclosed space and causing my nostrils to flare. I glanced over my shoulder to try and find the origin of the smell, and my heart quickened when my eyes met his again.

"Well, hello," he said, finally opening his mouth and speaking instead of just stealing quick glances in my direction.

"Hi," I said sheepishly.

His deep baritone awakened places that had been asleep for so long. I had been so focused on work that I hadn't made time for anything or anyone else. I had neglected my other needs, and it was a shame. It was a bigger shame that I was stepping foot on a plane to go bury my mother, and the only thing I could think of was getting naked with the stranger behind me. I walked down the aisle of the plane, but I noticed that the scent of his cologne seemed to be following me. The scent lingered because he was still behind me. I found my seat, and just with my luck he was seated right next to me. I laughed to myself as I slid my purse in the overhead compartment, and he waited patiently to be seated.

"I hate the window seat," he groaned.

"We can switch if you want," I suggested, "I don't mind."

"You sure?"

I nodded my head fervently and slid over to the window seat. He placed his carry-on in the overhead compartment and slid into the middle seat.

"I'm Lucas," he said, extending his hand in my direction.

"I'm Sundai."

He took my hand gingerly and shook it before the pilot made his pre-flight announcements.

"Good afternoon, ladies, and gentlemen. Welcome onboard flight 6B4 with service from LaGuardia to Montgomery Regional Airport with one stop at Charlotte Douglas International Airport. We are currently second in line for take-off and will be in the air in less than ten minutes. We ask that you go ahead and ensure that all baggage is secured in the overhead compartment, all seatbelts securely fastened, and all seats and trays in their upright position. Please power off all electronic devices or place them in airplane mode. Please keep in mind that smoking is prohibited for the duration of this flight. Thank you for traveling with us, and we hope that you enjoy your flight."

I quickly secured my seatbelt and watched as Lucas secured his. His pectoral muscles and abs seemed to be struggling to get out of his polo as he did. It may have been my imagination or my thirstiness that was making its way to the forefront. I wasn't sure, but either way, he looked damn good.

Fifteen minutes later, we were in the sky. I flagged down the flight attendant for a bag of peanuts and apple juice. It was a weird combination, but it always worked to soothe my flying jitters. I always joked with my mother that if God wanted me to fly, he would've given me wings. I was my happiest with both feet planted firmly on the ground, so I'd be lying if I said I wouldn't be happy when the flight was over.

"First time flying?" Lucas asked as he focused all of his attention on me.

His glance was captivating and made me feel like the plane was completely empty besides the two of us. I felt slightly nervous under his glance. Not the kind of nervousness that made me want to shy away, though. It was the kind of nervousness that made me want to get naked and feel the muscles that now seemed to be protruding from his clothing at an alarming rate. I laughed to myself. I was sure that it was my imagination, but the higher we flew, the sexier he became to me. My mouth watered for the not-so- stranger that sat next to me. I glanced out of the window in a frail attempt to keep myself from looking at him.

"I'm sorry," he said, his voice laced with defeat and sadness.

Okay, Sundai. You have to fly hours with this man. Let's not make this awkward. I thought to myself as I shifted in my seat to face him.

"No," I answered, "It's not my first flight, but I always get nervous."

He nodded his head as if he felt the same nerves that I did. He gave a reassuring smile, and I couldn't help but notice how straight and white his teeth were. It was something about a man with good hygiene that spoke to my soul.

"So, you have family in Alabama?" I asked.

"Actually, I do," he said, "my brother, Bryce, lives outside of Montgomery. I'm flying home to surprise him for my birthday."

"Wait," I said, "You are surprising *him* for *your* birthday?"

"Yea. We used to celebrate together, but the past few years work has kept me away, so I wanted to fly in and surprise him."

"That's sweet," I replied.

"What about you?" he asked, "What is bringing you to Alabama?"

"My mother passed," I answered woefully, and I noticed his expression change as well. I didn't mean to initiate a pity party on the plane. The chipper attitude that he displayed melted away and was replaced with caring eyes and an understanding disposition.

"I'm so sorry," he offered, "I've definitely been in that predicament."

"Really?"

"Yes, Bryce and I have lost both of our parents," he said, "So if anyone knows what you're going through, I do."

I appreciated the sympathy. Until that very moment, I hadn't spoken the words out loud, and admitting them only solidified them for me. A heaviness overcame my heart and tears welled in my eyes. I swallowed hard and attempted to push the feelings back down. The last thing I wanted to do was burst out crying in front of Lucas. I didn't know why I cared as much as I did. I would never see him again after the flight landed, but I still felt some type of way about crying in front of him.

"Hey," he said, placing his hand on my shoulder, "I'm sorry. I didn't mean to make you upset."

I scoffed that my emotions were as visible as they were. I never was successful when it came to hiding how I felt. The one day I was praying for a bit of secrecy I was extremely let down. Lucas sat in the seat next to me and read me like I was the Nadia Nicole novel I had tucked away in my carryon.

"I'm not upset," I lied.

"You are, and it's okay," he said as he moved his hand down my arm, "you're only human."

The feeling of him touching me seemed to send electricity through my entire body. We had a long flight to Alabama, and I prayed that I could keep my hormones in line until we got there. Then, I had every intention of getting off the plane and going far away from Lucas. Everything about him screamed trouble. Everything from the black and gold retro 12 Jordans on his feet, the crisply creased black jeans, fresh black t-shirt, and gold chain he wore should've run me in the other direction. If that didn't do it, the thick, full beard and crisply lined facial hair should have. His appearance screamed "player" or "ladies' man." He was too damn fine to be single, and I was sure he had a line of women as long as the plane we sat on, waiting to wet his beard. I appreciated his conversation and distraction during the ride. Once we were on the ground, he could go his way and I would go mine.

CHAPTER 4

Lucas

I flagged the flight attendant down as she walked down the aisle for what felt like the hundredth time. I was sure she was trying to catch my eye or the eye of some potential, unsuspecting bachelor. It wouldn't work for me though. The only thing she could do for me was bring me a drink and refill Sundai's snack of choice.

"Can I help you, sir?" She asked as she sauntered towards me.

"A rum and coke and peanuts and apple juice for her."

She turned to fulfill my request without another word, and I turned my attention back to Sundai. The glimmer in her eye evolved into a full-fledged blaze, and I saw it. I didn't know if our attraction was the same at this point, or if she was turned on by my take charge persona. We waited in silence for our drinks, and I took a long sip of mine before speaking again.

"So, do you have a man waiting for you in Alabama or back in New York?"

I studied every mannerism of her body, and the way she stiffened up instantly when I asked the question. It was as if it had put a sour taste in her mouth, and I hoped that I wasn't being too forward. I blamed my forwardness on my liquid courage and took another sip as I waited to see what her response was going to be.

To my surprise, she giggled a little. It was the slightest giggle, but it sounded like heaven to my ears. I imagined making her do that little sound on a regular basis.

"Nah," she finally responded, "no man."

A part of me wanted to pry and ask for more details, but I felt like she would tell me if and when she wanted to. I guess the apple juice was giving her courage as well, or maybe she was beginning to feel comfortable with me. Either way, she inhaled deeply and poured herself into our conversation.

"I focused all of my attention on my work," she explained, "I don't have time for love."

"Such a shame."

She snatched her head around and gazed out of the window. I could tell that her thoughts were a million miles away, but I didn't miss the curve in her cheeks when she smiled at my comment. She was putty in my hands, and I knew it. I didn't intend on boarding this flight to meet anyone, but it was something about Sundai that grabbed me by my soul, dick, and everything else. She grabbed me, and I wasn't sure I wanted her to let go. She was absolutely gorgeous, and her aura was gravitational. She sucked me into her orbit, and I wanted to do things to her that she could never imagine. She was torn between the view outside of the window and watching me. I didn't envy her one bit. Flying always seemed to give me anxiety, and I needed no reminder of how high we were flying. I didn't care to see the miniature buildings and landscapes as we flew by. Normally, I would have earbuds in listening to something, but I didn't want to come across rude. I figured we would spark a decent conversation on the flight, and honestly, I was open to it.

"What are you doing on the layover?" I asked her as she stole another glance in my direction.

"I hadn't planned anything," she admitted, "What are you doing?"

"You."

Her eyes bulged to at least twice their normal size when I let the word fall carelessly out of my mouth. The liquor definitely had me feeling ballsy as hell, but she didn't seem to mind. She held my gaze for longer than necessary, and I stared right back into her chocolate orbs. I could see and feel everything. I felt like I was swimming in an endless sea of Sundai, and I didn't care. I just waded there. I swam past the hurt of losing her mother. I swam past the walls and barriers put there by a man who didn't love her the way she needed to be loved. I swam right past the barricades she tried to erect to protect herself and her feelings. I kept right on plunging until I was face-to-face with a beast. It had been chained up and tucked away, but flying over Virginia, I had the pleasure of meeting her. She was ravenous for my attention, and her eyes said it all. She needed me as much as I wanted her, and I had every intention of obliging her.

An hour later, the plane landed safely at Charlotte Douglas International Airport. I all but ran off the plane. I had put a bug in Sundai's ear to meet me in the handicap bathroom if she was about that life. I headed in that direction, and I wondered if she would be joining me.

CHAPTER 5

Sundai

"This man is out of his damn mind,"** I thought to myself as the plane touched ground in North Carolina. He had a complete plan for me, and all I had to do was show up. He was going to take me down in the handicap bathroom of the airport like I was a cheap whore or a quick jump off. A part of me felt offended that he approached me like that, but a bigger part of me felt ridiculous for wanting to go along with his plan. I wanted to run into that bathroom and leave my cares and inhibitions behind me. I imagined walking into that bathroom and feeling his skin merge with mine. I sat in my seat on the plane and briefly closed my eyes. I imagined his lips delicately stroking my skin as he placed kisses all over me. I envisioned him positioned between my thighs ready to claim my sex as his own. It had been almost two years since I had sex, and I knew that I would be a little rusty. Hell, I didn't remember what it felt like or what to do. Lucas stared at me hungrily like he was ready to knock the dust off that thang if I let him.

The captain rattled off a series of announcements that I couldn't comprehend. I was too enthralled with the dark chocolate, God of a man that sat in the seat next to me. He commanded my attention, and I willingly gave it to him. I bit down on my bottom lip as I pictured him bending me over the counter in the bathroom. A heat rush encamped my body and sweat beads trickled down my forehead. He took his thumb and gingerly pulled my lip out of my mouth.

"Don't do that," he growled.

After what felt like forever, we were released from the plane, and we walked towards the main waiting area of the airport. My heart thumped to its own cadence as we walked, and my breathing increased. I felt like I would hyperventilate at any moment, and I struggled to keep my composure. I was horny as hell, but I didn't need that on full display as I trotted past strangers who were waiting on this layover like we were. The airport was full of people and buzzing with activity. I watched as unsuspecting strangers passed me and went along their way. Some settled into vinyl chairs while others waited in line to get a snack. Lucas' eyes scanned the waiting area before they met mine. Unspoken messages were transferred. He was feet away from where I stood, but I under-stood exactly what he was telling me. A sly smile spread across his face as the door slid closed behind him. I had a moment of insanity as my feet moved in that direction. I glanced around to see if anyone was paying an ounce of attention to me. They were all focused on what they had going on. No one even glanced in the direction of the thot that was making her way through the airport. No one even knew that I was seconds away from making one of the biggest mistakes of my life. I made my way across the stale, gray tile floor, and I was inches away from the door before my feet paused. I stood frozen in thought as I envisioned what was waiting for me on the other side of the door. I inhaled deeply and pushed all of the hot, amorous thoughts to the back of my mind. I shook my head intently as if the thoughts would up and fall out of my ears. I secretly wished they would fall out of my ears and roll across the floor—far, far away from me. I stood for a few more moments basking in the scent of Lucas' cologne that lingered by the door before I gave up. I came to my senses, turned on my heels, and got the hell away from that door. I knew what going inside would mean, but I wouldn't find out—not in this lifetime.

Instead, I sashayed my ass right up to the airport's transfer desk. Lucas had a plan, but I had one of my own.

"Hello. May I help you?" A blonde-haired woman with the bluest eyes I had ever seen asked.

Her name tag read, Sky, which I thought to be a fitting name. I stared at her eyes for a moment before I deemed it to be awkward and willed myself to speak.

"Sorry," I said, "I was trying to see if you guys had another flight to Montgomery, Alabama that I could transfer to."

"Is something wrong with the flight you are on?" She asked.

I wanted to say, "hell yes" and go into every detail of what I was feeling. Instead, I settled for a brief, "sort of."

She didn't ask any more questions, which was fine by me. Less questions meant less information I had to give up. I managed to save myself further embarrassment as she typed on the keyboard in front of her. Moments ticked by like hours as I waited for her response. I quickly prayed that she would come up with something before Lucas figured out that I wasn't joining him.

"Actually, there is one that is boarding now. Take off is in twenty minutes," she informed me, "If we hurry, you can make it."

"Great."

I stood patiently as she typed a few more things into the computer and passed me a new ticket. I took off in the direction of the new gate for my new flight, but not before I glanced back towards that bathroom. Lucas had finally grown restless with waiting and emerged. He stood in the lobby looking puzzled and slightly annoyed. I picked up the pace before he could spot me, and before I knew it, I was on the boarding bridge. Every care I had melted away as I settled into a new seat next to a frail, silver-haired woman. My hormones settled back into whatever cavern they emerged from as we took off towards Alabama.

CHAPTER 6

Bryce

I woke up the next morning with a wet beard, and a hundred-pound mastiff staring into my eyes. I blinked several times to clear the fog that had settled in my brain. Apparently, I wasn't moving fast enough for Kane, though. Before I could react, his tongue was out licking my cheek again. The whine that accompanied the lick let me know that his situation was urgent, and he wanted to go outside sooner than later. I slinked out of bed and slid my feet into the pair of Adidas slides that were parked next to my bed. I bypassed my morning cup of coffee, attached Kane's leash, and headed right out of the door. The rays from the early morning sun felt good on my exposed skin as we walked down the sidewalk. He paused to handle his business, and I stared aimlessly at Mrs. Opal's house. I couldn't believe that she was gone. A part of me wanted to go knock on her door and see what she was cooking for breakfast. I wanted to grab one of her homemade buttermilk biscuits and pear preserve to pair with my coffee. I had a jar of preserves in my cabinet, but I seriously doubted that I could make the biscuits as good as she did. She would stand at her kitchen island and roll them to heavenly perfection. Even in her old age and failing health, she managed to throw down in the kitchen.

"Cooking speaks to my soul," she would say, "I love seeing the smile on people's faces when they eat my food."

A lone tear slid down the side of my face, and I didn't bother to swipe it away. I let it roll and fall wherever it wanted to. Kane wrapped up his business and headed directly back towards my front door. I imagined that his stomach was as empty as mine, and I understood the assignment. I pulled two old plastic bowls from the cabinet. I filled one with his food and the other with water before placing them in the middle of the kitchen floor. I expected him to hesitate or feel slightly unsure in the new environment, but the mastiff in him took over. He began to devour the pedigree as I brewed a cup of coffee.

Two hours later, we were well fed and watching television when I heard a car door close. Kane's ears perked up so that I knew I had not imagined it.

"Let's go, boy," I said as I grabbed his leash and headed towards the door.

A red Toyota Corolla sat in Mrs. Opal's driveway, and a body was leaned over in the trunk. I couldn't see the face, but the body was curvaceous and thick in the right places. Even in her jogging pants and sneakers, I could tell that she was legit.

"Hello?" I asked as the dog and I got closer.

The last thing I wanted to do was startle whoever it was. She stood up, and my suspicions were confirmed. She had a face to match the body I admired from afar. She resembled a twenty-year younger version of Mrs. Opal, so I felt safe to assume that it was her daughter. The pictures inside of the house did her absolutely no justice at all. I felt my breathing quicken as I stared at her. It was the weirdest feeling I had ever experienced in my life. I was a decent looking man, and I never had a hard time with the females, but it was something about this one that left me dumbfounded and speechless. She must have felt something as well because she stood staring at me for a brief moment before she diverted her attention to Kane.

"There you are," she said as she reached out and rubbed his head, "I've been looking all over for you."

"He ran out yesterday when the ambulance came," I informed her as I passed the leash to her, "You must be Sundai."

"Thank you, and yes I am."

She tugged at a suitcase in the trunk of the car, but the weight of the bag combined with Kane's weight proved to be more of a struggle than she imagined. The man in me stepped right up to the plate to help her.

"Here," I said as I grabbed the bag out of the trunk, "let me."

"Um, who are you again?"

She stood with Kane's leash in one hand and the other hand resting firmly on her hip. Her hair was pulled into a tight ponytail, and her face was bare except for the lip gloss on her lips. Her eyes were full of emotion, and I could instantly see the relationship between her and her mother. She had definitely inherited every ounce of spunk and spice Mrs. Opal had. That apple didn't fall far from that tree at all.

"Sorry," I corrected, "I'm Bryce, your mother's next-door neighbor."

"You mean you used to be her neighbor."

I nodded my head solemnly. I still refused to speak of Mrs. Opal in past tense. I know that I couldn't bring her back, but I didn't feel the need to rub it in either. She took the dog and trotted towards the front door. I rolled her suitcase up the sidewalk behind her. I struggled to keep my eyes glued to the back of her head. Her curves were voluptuous, and her ass was swollen and bulging out of the back of her pants. It seemed to be calling to me, but I refused to indulge in even the quickest glance.

"Thank you," she said as she reached the front door and let Kane inside.

"You're welcome. Do you need anything else?"

"Well," she started, "Since you are offering, I have to start packing up my mother's stuff."

"Say less."

CHAPTER 7
Sundai

I couldn't believe that I had invited an almost complete stranger in to help me pack up my mother's belongings. I had always heard about the fine man that lived next door to her. She would always call me and tell me about some dinner they had together, or how he was out there mowing the lawn or planting flowers for her. She knew him well, and he seemed to be a place holder of sorts until I got home. One thing about it, Opal Mae was a good judge of character. If he made it past Kane and Opal, he would be good with me.

"Can I get you something to drink or a snack?" I asked as we were nestled inside of the house.

"Not unless you have some of your mother's buttermilk biscuits tucked away somewhere," he said with a wide grin.

His statement caused me to grin as well. I knew exactly what he was talking about and the feeling that those biscuits evoked. She had been making them for me every Sunday morning since I was a little girl, and tears filled my eyes as my mind strolled down memory lane.

"I can't believe that she is really gone," I said in a voice barely audible over a whisper.

"Hey," he said, moving across the room until he was at my side, "I didn't mean to make you cry."

When the distance closed between us, the oxygen seemed to be sucked out of the room. He was handsome to say the least. It was something about his smooth, chocolate skin that resonated in my soul. His tall, muscular frame looked like it was ready to snatch me up and hold on to me for the rest of forever. He looked oddly familiar to me, but I couldn't quite place where I may have known him from. I shook my uncertainties away as I pulled out some boxes that I stopped and bought on the way to the house.

I passed Bryce the unassembled boxes and roll of shipping tape and watched him go right to work building the boxes. I stood and watched in awe as the manly man in him took over. I knew that he was building boxes not building a house or some other complicated tasks, but I still studied the way he worked. He was good with his hands, and I could tell from standing there watching him.

A few hours later, we had the majority of my mom's things packed up. I packed what I wanted to keep and made separate piles to be taken to Goodwill or the homeless women's shelter downtown. I plopped down on the couch, swiping at loose strands of hair that managed to escape the ponytail that I thought was tight. I took a few deep breaths to try and control the panic attack that was brewing inside of me. My mother was really gone, and I couldn't believe it. I wasn't here to hold her hand when she transitioned, and it bothered me. Guilt consumed me as I looked around at what was left of her house. She sacrificed so much so I could manifest my dreams. She hustled extremely hard, so that I wouldn't have to. Opal deserved the world, and I wasn't around to give it to her. The mere thought ate away at my conscience, and it upset my stomach.

"Penny for your thoughts," Bryce spoke, interrupting the pity party I was secretly throwing.

I glanced up from my spot on the couch to see him taping the last box. His expression was sincere and concerned. It was endearing to have someone actually care about how I felt.

"Sorry, I'm back with you now."

"You never left, but I could tell that your mind was definitely somewhere else."

"I was just thinking about mama. She was my everything and now she's gone," I admitted.

The mourning and sadness came in waves. At one point in time, I was fine. I managed to smile and carry on. The next minute I was down in the dumps and ready to fall apart. It was a normal part of grieving. I knew that, but I never imagined that I would be going through this so soon. Opal was sick for a while, and I knew that the end was near. Nothing would have prepared me for it though, and I was eternally grateful that I didn't have to deal with it alone. It was a chance encounter that I ran into Bryce, but I silently thanked God for his presence.

"She's not suffering anymore," Bryce said quietly, "that is cause for happiness."

As right as he was, it didn't make me feel much better. I smiled slightly. It was a fake smile that I forced myself to plaster onto my face, and I knew it. I guess it was enough for Bryce because he moved right along with the conversation.

"So, you need something to take your mind off of everything," he said.

"Something like what?"

"Let me take you out to dinner or something," he said, "I would love to get to know you."

It sounded like a good idea. I hadn't been on a date in forever, and according to Opal this meeting was written in the stars. She always bragged about the handsome neighbor that lived next to her. She claimed we needed to meet sooner than later, and we would have some beautiful children. I always rolled my eyes and smacked my lips when she started talking about him, and a part of me hated that we missed the opportunity to be under the same roof with her at the same time. I figured that she was in heaven having a good "I told you so" moment and a fit of laughter at our expense.

"Any other time, I would love to," I told him, "but I really need to be concentrating on planning Opal's homegoing."

"The plans will be there. It's just a meal, and I know you haven't eaten yet," he insisted.

I had no idea how he knew, but I hadn't eaten. It felt like my stomach was touching my back. Even though I was starving, it didn't feel right to have my mind on anything other than Opal's funeral service. She had everything planned and written down, so there wasn't much left for me to do. All I had to do was call the funeral home and set the ball into motion. So, even though a part of me was telling me to run in the other direction, I nodded my head slowly. I beat myself up for agreeing to it. I felt like I was somehow betraying my mother. I took a slow glance around the house. I was hoping someone snapped their fingers, and I woke up from this nightmare. Opal was supposed to be sitting in her recliner playing matchmaker between Bryce and me. I could hear her laugh in the back of my head as Bryce stared me down waiting for a reaction from me.

"Look," he finally spoke, "If it's too awkward, we can make it a double date."

A puzzled look crept over my face. I didn't have any friends in Alabama that I could call on the whim for a double date. I assumed that he knew someone, and the thought of another female being present made me feel a lot better. I exhaled slowly as he proceeded to explain.

"My brother and whatever female he's dating at the moment can join us."

CHAPTER 8

Bryce

I watched Sundai move methodically through her mother's house. She was a woman on a mission. She didn't seem to be grieving. I never saw her break down or take a moment to cry. No tears cascaded against her smooth skin, and it worried me for a moment. She was a robot without any feelings or attachments, and that fact alone scared me. I wondered if she was bottling all of her emotions behind an emotional dam that would burst at any given second. If so, I made a mental note to be there for her when her emotions overflowed.

I didn't know what it was about her, but I wanted to be there for her. I wanted to be in her presence. I felt like I would do or be whatever she needed me to. I just met her, but I never wanted to let her go. I never wanted to be without her. I wanted to inhale her oxygen, feel every inch of her glorious skin, and be all up and through her personal space. I felt dazed and confused about the feelings that were surging through me. I never had the desire to entertain women. I kept my head down and focused on my job, but it was something about Sundai. Maybe it was the confidence that seemed to seep from her pores. Maybe it was the glow that seemed to radiate from her, or maybe it was some crazy juju that

Mrs. Opal had going on. I wasn't sure, but whatever it was had me smitten and there wasn't anything I could do about it.

She stared off into space as if her mind was jam-packed with thoughts. I wanted to dissect her mind and find out what made her tick.

"What's wrong now?"

"Everything," she replied somberly.

"I get it, love. I really do."

She inhaled deeply and took her time blowing the breath out. A part of me felt bad for her. I knew how it felt to lose people. It hurt like hell especially when there was no closure. I wanted to jump up and hold her in my arms, but I refrained.

"Listen," I said to her, "it may not seem like it, but everything will be okay. My grandmother used to say that weeping may endure for a night, but joy comes in the morning."

She scoffed lightly. I knew that she probably couldn't see any joy in this situation, and I kicked myself for saying it. In my head, it fits the situation. Out loud it didn't make much sense, but I tried.

"So," she spoke, interrupting my thoughts, "When are we going to eat?"

"Let me go put some clothes on and we can go," I said, "How about an hour?"

She nodded her head in agreement, and I turned to head back to my house.

"Thank you," she said to my back.

"Anytime," I tossed over my shoulder. I said it, meant it, and I hoped that she knew it.

CHAPTER 9

Lucas

"That's it. Right there," I growled into the ear of the tenderoni I was balls deep inside of.

She was matching my stride stroke for stroke. I stared at her curvaceous hips and ass as she threw it back in my direction. I had her bent over the couch in my suite. The only thing I knew about her was that her name was Alaisha, and she was the night manager at the hotel I was staying in. She was there the first night I checked in, and she couldn't keep her eyes off of me. She stared at me like I was a piece of prime rib fresh off somebody's grill. The only thing that was missing was a trail of drool from her luscious, glossed lips. I knew as soon as I saw them that they'd be wrapped around me soon. I knew instantly that she was going to be spreading her legs somewhere in this hotel for me. She screamed sex, and I welcomed it since I was ghosted at the airport.

"Yes daddy! Fuck your pussy," she yelled, pulling me back to the current moment.

I wasn't sure when I became daddy or when I took ownership of her pussy, but it didn't stop me from assaulting her woman hood. I delivered long, deep soul-stirring strokes as Alaisha gripped the throw pillows on the couch for dear life. Her moans seemed to echo around the room as I felt her vagina pulsate around my shaft. I knew she was on the verge of exploding, and I wanted to get every bit of her orgasm out. I quickened my stroke as I grabbed her hips. I guided her down my dick until her ass slapped against my stomach. The jiggle that reverberated across her skin seemed unreal. In my mind, it may have been. I couldn't tell if she was blessed with the curves, or if she paid for them. The thought crossed my mind momentarily, but her pending orgasm pulled me back to the room with her.

"Give me that shit," I growled, "Stop holding back."

"I'm not," she whimpered.

"Cum for me."

On cue, I felt her tighten more than ever before. The pressure from her squeeze drove me up a wall. She released me and I erupted shortly after.

She went into the restroom, I assumed to clean herself up, as I sat on the very couch we had just got done fucking on. Whispers of the scent of her sex lingered in the air. I took a deep breath and attempted to hold on to the memory of how her body felt. I pulled a pack of cigarettes from my pocket but didn't get to light one. "The Best Man I Can Be" by Ginuwine, R.L., Tyrese, and Case interrupted my thoughts. It was my brother, Bryce's, ringtone so I felt like it was imperative that I answer.

"Yo."

"Yo man," his voice resounded over the phone, "What are you up to?"

"Just climbing out of some pussy," I admitted.

"Really? You just got into town," he said, stating the obvious.

"It kind of just landed in my lap," I said, "and I've never been one to turn down some free ass."

He laughed at my statement, but we both knew that it was the truth. He was more of the romantic type. I wasn't. I fucked them and ghosted them. I was a player of sorts, and it didn't bother me one bit. My mind wandered to the fine ass woman that stood me up in the airport bathroom. She was going to be another name on my list, but I didn't get the chance to. I wasn't due to be at my brother's house until later that evening, so I knew that he was calling me for some reason.

"What's up?" I asked, trying to pry the reason out of him.

"You wanna go out and get a bite to eat later?"

"Hell yea."

"One thing though," he said.

I inhaled a sharp breath. I wondered what he was up to. It was always some shit with Bryce, so I braced myself for whatever it was he was about to say.

"I met this woman that I am really feeling. I wanted to take her out, but she's more comfortable with a double date. I was hoping that you could help a brother out."

"Help you out how?" I asked slightly irritated, "Where am I supposed to find a date? It's so last minute."

"Hell, bring whatever woman you were just bumping uglies with."

"This wasn't that, but I'll ask her."

We disconnected the call, and I waited patiently for Alaisha to emerge from the bathroom. I heard the water turn off, so I braced myself to tell her about what Bryce had called about. She slinked out of the restroom, and for the first time I noticed how gorgeous she really was. Her skin resembled a Hershey's chocolate bar. It was smooth, blemish-free, and had a sort of glow to it. Her hair fell easily below her shoulder blades, and her body was banging. I could see myself dating and fucking her on a regular basis. It put a sour taste in my mouth that I fucked her off the rip, but that was as much as her decision as it was mine.

"What's on your mind, handsome?" She purred as she plopped down on the couch next to me.

"Wanna go on a date?"

Her eyes swelled to the size of half dollars, and she smiled wide enough to show off all thirty-two of her teeth. They were straight and white which was an automatic turn on for me. I knew her mind was reeling because she didn't expect me to ask her that. Honestly, I didn't imagine asking her either, but for Bryce I would move heaven and hell.

"Where too?" She asked me.

"My brother and his date invited me to a double dinner with them this evening," I explained to her.

"Oh, so you just asked because you needed a date?"

"Nah, I asked you because I wanted to. I could've asked anyone."

The expression on her face instantly changed. Her lips pursed, and her attitude began to show its ugly face. I didn't feel like going back and forth with her. She could keep that shit. Women came a dime a dozen. Just like she came, someone else would come too.

"Do you want to go or not?"

She nodded her head without saying a word. *That's what the fuck I thought.*

CHAPTER 10

Bryce

T he vibe in the restaurant was welcoming. The crowd was small, and the lighting was dim and ambient. I had never been to Chill before, but I had heard about the spot. It had only been open a few months, but it had managed to become the talk of the town. Chill was being talked about in the barbershop, the grocery store, and even on the radio. I decided that it would be the perfect backdrop for Sundai and me to get to know each other.

People were seated sporadically around the bar, so I opted for a seat that was kind of secluded on the other side of the restaurant. The sky-blue plush velvet couches that encircled the table screamed elegance, and the smile that spread across Sundai's face let me know that I had made the right decision. I was glad to think that she was finally lightening up a little bit. I had to fight her tooth and nail to get her to ride to the restaurant with me. In my mind, it didn't make sense for us to leave the same street headed to the same destination in two cars. I guess in her mind, I was some psycho woman killer that was going to abduct her instead of wine and dine her. My only agenda was to see the smile that was currently lighting up the restaurant. When I said I was feeling her, I meant it. Doing harm to her was the furthest thing from my mind. Unless, I had her face down ass up in my bed, but that would come later—much later.

I slid into one side of the booth and watched intently as Sundai studied for a moment before sliding in next to me. The look on her face was one of nervousness and shyness mixed into one with a ribbon on it. The server took our drink orders and left us to have our own conversation.

"A lemon drop martini, huh?" I asked as soon as the server was out of earshot.

"Yep. I'm a fan of all things sour. Plus, the vodka will knock the edge off things."

I knew when she said "knock the edge off things" that she was referring to her nerves, and I said a silent prayer that the drink would help. Moments later our server, Mariangel, returned with a lemon drop martini and a bourbon lemonade.

"Thank you, Mariangel," I said politely, brandishing her a smile as well.

"Please call me Mari," she replied, "are you guys ready to order?"

"We're waiting on the rest of our party."

"Sure thing. I'll check back in a few minutes."

I nodded my head intently and watched as she walked away.

"So, tell me about Sundai," I interjected into the silence before it could overcome us.

"What is there to tell?"

"Anything you find interesting," I told her, and I was serious. I wanted to know it all.

"Well, I'm sure my mother probably told you all there was to know about me, but here goes," she started.

We spent the next thirty minutes chatting, and I learned everything there was to know about her. Everything from her favorite color being yellow to her dream of being married, having four kids, a huge house, and a labradoodle. The conversation flowed smoothly, and it made me feel like we had known each other our entire lives.

"So, where's whoever you invited?" she asked suspiciously.

"He's supposed to be here by now," I admitted, "but he'd be late to his own funeral if the pallbearers weren't carrying him."

CHAPTER 11

Lucas

"Heifer, come on," I screamed from the living room space of the suite.

I instantly regretted inviting her. We were late for the date with Bryce, and she insisted on taking another shower. Sure, I had brought her to countless orgasms throughout the day but when I told her to be dressed and ready to go by six-thirty I meant just that. I was already starting to see that Alaisha and I wouldn't make it as a couple. We were too different. I was water and she was oil, and she wasn't an expensive Crisco type oil either. She was the cheap Piggly Wiggly brand that you bought when you were down to your last few dollars. I was a lot of things, but late was never one of them. I believed in punctuality as it was drilled in my head by my grandfather. He was in the military, so even if you were early, you were late.

I was fully dressed in a black Yves Saint Laurent dress shirt and matching pants. My shoes were black as well, and the only contrast to the black-on-black attire was the silver jewelry that I wore. A white gold, diamond encrusted Patek Philippe watch hung from my right wrist. The face was black like everything else I wore. A fourteen-karat stud rested in my right ear that coordinated perfectly with the cross that hung loosely around my neck. I debated about whether or not to wear my VVS encrusted grill as well. A part of me didn't care that much because I didn't feel like Alaisha was worth it. A bigger part of me couldn't help myself. I was slightly narcissistic and felt like any time I stepped out of the house I had to be put together. I didn't give a damn where I went or who I went with. Lucas was going to show up and show the fuck out. I wanted every female in the place to cream their panties when they saw me. I wanted every man in the place to want to be me.

I checked out my appearance in the mirror next to the door as I waited impatiently for Alaisha to emerge from the bathroom. I prayed that she looked like something when she came out. A few minutes later she came out, and I was thoroughly surprised. She was dressed in a black floor-length maxi dress that featured a bouquet of roses that started at the top of the dress and wrapped around the length of the dress to the bottom. Her hair was pulled up into a tight bun with a few loose curls hanging on each side of her face. Her makeup was light but worked well to accentuate her features. She was beautiful to say the least, and it instantly made me eat my words. She was definitely not the cheap oil. She was extra virgin olive oil, and I needed every drop of her in my life.

"You ready?" she asked in a quiet voice.

I couldn't vocalize anything, so I simply nodded my head and held the door open for her.

Twenty minutes later, we pulled up to Chill. I had heard of the restaurant, but I had never been there before. I was surprised that Bryce picked this location for a first date. It was extremely upscale, and I knew he was trying to impress whoever this woman was.

She better be worth this shit. I thought to myself as I pulled my rental car into the valet circle.

The valet attendant opened Alaisha's door, but she didn't move. She didn't budge from the car until I made my way around to her side and extended my arm in her direction. She gracefully intertwined her arm in mine, and her chunky wedge sandals made contact with the sidewalk in front of Chill.

From the outside, we looked like a power couple. Our stride gave off boss energy, and we captured the attention of everyone we passed. All eyes were on us, and I loved it. I held the door open for Alaisha and as we stepped inside, the décor took me by surprise. The sky blue and silver that was sprinkled around the room reminded me of ice. I guess it was meant to coordinate with the name of the place.

I scanned the room for my brother and found him nestled up in the corner of the restaurant. He was skinning and grinning in her face, and I could read his emotions a mile away. He was smitten with this unknown woman, and she seemed just as smitten with him. We approached the table where they were seated, and I froze in my tracks. My blood boiled feverishly in my veins as I stared from my brother to the woman, he was kee-keeing with. Apparently, Bryce didn't notice the look on my face as he proceeded with introducing me to the woman I already knew.

"Bruh, it's about time you got here," he started.

"This is my brother, Lucas," he said motioning in my direction, "and this is—"

"Sundai," I spoke matter-of-factly, interrupting him.

The look on Bryce's face tickled me as I slid into the booth across from them. Alaisha slid in next to me, but a hole could've opened in the floor and swallowed her up. I would've cared in the least bit. My focus was solely on Sundai. I hadn't seen her since our rendezvous on the plane, and it irked my nerves to see her sitting in this restaurant with my brother of all people.

"Sundai Johnson," Alaisha said with a smirk.

Her head tilted to the side as she waited for Sundai to recognize her. Bryce and I sat looking like two fools trying to figure out what in the hell was going on.

CHAPTER 12
Sundai

Everything was going so well. My drink was well mixed, and the conversation between Bryce and I went smoothly. He was a really nice guy, and it was a nice change to take my mind off of the grief that was overcoming my mind. Everything was perfect, but of course perfect doesn't exist. It was just my luck that the person we were waiting on was the same person I bailed on on the way to Alabama. My throat felt like it was closing as I struggled to breathe. I wanted to keep my composure while sitting next to Bryce, but my insides were a mess. Not only was he here, but he was here with Alaisha Thompson. I hadn't seen her in over twenty years, but nothing had changed about her. She still had the same hourglass figure and the same smug aura about herself.

"Well, hello," I said to no one in particular.

"How do you know them?" Bryce asked, slightly confused.

"I met Sundai at the airport on the way here," Lucas answered me.

I prayed that he didn't divulge any more details, and luckily my prayers were answered because he left it at that. I wasn't sure for how long though, and I felt like I was treading on thin ice dealing with Bryce and Lucas. I didn't like it one bit. I wanted to run far away from them both and never look back.

"Understood," Bryce spoke up again, "But how do you know his date?"

"Alaisha and I went to high school together," I said through pursed lips.

"Oh, that's it? We just went to high school together?" She asked with an irritated roll of her neck.

The air in the restaurant seemed to have dropped a few degrees, and I shuddered. I was being put on the spot from all angles, and I didn't like it. I wanted to get up and leave them all sitting at the table, but I didn't have anything to feel guilty or ashamed about. So, I sat there. I sat there under the watchful eyes of Lucas and the overwhelming attitude from Alaisha.

"What this bitch is failing to mention is that we used to be best friends in high school," she spat callously.

"Yea, we *used* to be," I responded, ignoring her casual use of the word bitch. I wasn't going to be too many more of her bitches though. If she let the word fall out of her mouth again, I didn't mind dragging her out of the restaurant and across the entire parking lot. I wasn't a fighter, but I had been through too much over the past couple of days to deal with her trifling ass.

"What happened?" Lucas asked, interrupting my thought process, "Why aren't y'all friends anymore?"

"We aren't friends because the uppity bitch decided to turn her back on where she came from. She got high and mighty like she wasn't playing hide and seek in the same projects I was playing in."

The sound of her voice sounded like nails on a chalkboard to me. Everything about her and her presence irritated me. I made up my mind that I was going to try to sit through lunch and not say anything. I was going to be cordial as long as she was cordial, but it was too late for that. She kept poking at the sleeping bear inside of me, and I was about to unleash it on her ass. Sure, I was composed Sundai Johnson who sat in front of a camera and reported news every day, but deep inside, I was still "Dai Dai." I was still the little nappy headed girl that struggled to pull her hair into two ponytails. I was still from the Hillman Crest projects, as she was trying her hardest to remind me. Truth be told, I never forgot. I knew exactly where I came from, and I strived to become a better person and make a better life for myself. I tried hard to get out of the trenches, and Alaisha was about to drag me right back through them.

"Listen," I said and paused as I gathered myself for what I was about to say to her.

"You are the same jealous, miserable something you were when we graduated high school. The only reason you are mad at me is because I chose to make something of myself. I chose not to stay around Hillman, and I definitely decided not to start sucking dick and selling ass for McDonald's."

Her lips flew open like she had something to say, but I held up my hand stopping any sound that she could have produced. I wasn't done. She had asked for this, and she was going to hear every word that I had to say. I was done when I said I was done, and not a second sooner.

"We were friends, so you would think that *my friend* would be happy for me. You would think that *my friend* would be in my corner cheering me on. Instead, you've had my name in your mouth ever since I chose to go away to college. You have hated every decision I made, and that alone lets me know you were never my friend. You were an opp in sheep's clothing. Fuck you and everything you stand for at this point. I don't care if you like me or not."

At this point, my voice was loud, and the few patrons in the restaurant had turned their heads in our direction. I was causing a slight disturbance, but I didn't give a damn. Bryce reached out and placed his hand on my upper thigh. The embrace was comforting and reassuring. Through it all, he was on my side, and I appreciated it.

"Bitch," she started defensively.

"Her name is Sundai," Bryce said, "refer to her as such or don't address her at all."

His voice was a flawless mixture of acidity and firmness. He lacked a threatening undertone, but everyone at the table could tell that he meant what he had said. A part of me was surprised that he had opened his mouth to say anything. I had literally just met him and agreed to this dinner, and he already felt compelled to defend me. I felt honored to be sitting at the table next to him.

"Yea shorty," Lucas interjected, "You have been dropping those bitch bombs left and right—highly disrespectful. You need to check your attitude and apologize. I don't give a damn about what happened in the past. She hasn't done anything to you today."

I felt my bottom lip fly away from my top one. Both brothers were speaking up in my defense, and I was sitting there like a deer in headlights. I didn't know what to say or what to do.

"Disrespectful? Let's talk about disrespect. She just sat here and said I was sucking dick and selling ass for McDonald's?"

"Well, were you?" Lucas grilled.

A giggle stirred up from my soul, but I tried my hardest to swallow it back down. Only two people at the table knew the truth, and I wondered if she was going to be honest or if she was going to put on airs in front of them like she was the perfect angel. I waited on bated breath as Bryce took a sip of his Bourbon lemonade.

"It wasn't even McDonald's," she said, "It was Golden Corral."

Bryce choked on his drink as she said the words, and the giggle that I struggled to contain bubbled its way up my throat before I finally exploded in a fit of laughter. Lucas's eyes seemed to be about to pop out of his head at any given moment, and I waited patiently to see how he was going to handle the news.

"Sundai, I was never jealous of you—not intentionally," Alaisha spoke after a few minutes, "Everyone wasn't as well off as you were. I didn't have a mother that worked endlessly to make sure I had what I needed. My father raped my sister and I, so he wasn't any help either."

"What?"

"Yea. When we graduated, I just knew we would be going together. Instead, you pulled off and left me in your smoke. I wasn't jealous. I was heartbroken," she admitted.

I retracted every evil and vile thing I had thought of her before. The revelation she shared shattered my heart into a million pieces. I never knew. I never asked. I just figured it was one of those things where people grow up, move away, and go on their separate paths. I knew there were some hard feelings and animosity, but I never knew any of what she revealed today.

I rose from the table, and she instantly rose from her side. I extended my arms in her direction until she slid into my embrace. She rested her head on my shoulder and the hunching of her shoulders was a key indication that she was crying. I instinctively rubbed her back as we stood in the middle of the restaurant holding each other. It didn't matter where we were. Once upon a time, the woman in my arms was like a sister to me. We were so in sync that our cycles came at the same time. We went through every break-up, make-up, and everything together. She was my ace, and I was hers. Memories flooded my mind as we stood in Chill.

"I'm so sorry," I said barely above a whisper, "I'm so sorry."

I glanced over her top knot bun to see Lucas looking on with a hungry expression on his face. I didn't like it one bit. It made me feel like we were meat and he was a starving tiger ready to pounce and kill.

"Well," he finally spoke up, "Isn't this just cute. Now we can all eat and go home and have a foursome."

I wasn't sure if he was joking or serious, but either way his comment repulsed me. I released Alaisha, and we returned to our seats. Twenty minutes later, they had drinks, we had refills and food was being delivered to our table.

"I'm glad you decided to come," Bryce said to me.

I nodded my head, but before I could say anything Lucas spoke up.

"Me too. So, we can finish what we started."

"What is he talking about?" Bryce asked me.

I hunched my shoulders in a lie. I knew exactly what he was referring to, but I couldn't believe that he even brought it up in front of his brother. He knew I was there as Bryce's date, but apparently that piece of information didn't matter one bit. Alaisha and I began to dig into our food as the brothers hashed it out.

"What the hell are you talking about?" Bryce directed his line of questioning towards his brother.

"She didn't tell you what happened at the airport, huh?"

I dropped my fork, and the clanging of metal and porcelain rang throughout the restaurant. I could feel the color draining from my face. It felt like Lucas had a vice grip on my lungs and every word he spoke squeezed tighter and tighter. I was asthmatic as a child, and this encounter was definitely giving me asthma vibes. I couldn't breathe. My fight or flight instincts were revving on ten again, and the only thing I could think of was getting out.

"I have to go," I all but screamed as I jumped up from the table.

CHAPTER 13

Bryce

Confusion coursed through my brain. I had no idea what was going on, and I wasn't sure that I wanted to know. I knew my brother's reputation as a man, but from my understanding the two had just met at the airport. She didn't know who he was or that we were related so I wouldn't hold anything against her. Lucas on the other hand kept pushing the issue and making statements that were borderline disrespectful. The tension at our table was so thick that I could've picked it up and tossed it. All I wanted to do was enjoy my shrimp and grits, sip my drink, and enjoy everyone's company. I knew that it was over though. It was confirmed when Sundai jumped up from the table in a frenzy.

"I have to go," she said.

"Let's get out of here, then," I told her.

"Your brother is here. I'll catch an Uber or something."

"The hell you say. I invited you out, I am responsible for making sure you get home safely."

She opened her mouth to object again, but our eyes connected first. The look on my face let her know that this discussion was not a debate. I wasn't the abusive or aggressive type, but I had morals and standards. She came with me, and she was leaving with me. I pulled out a wad of bills and tossed them to Lucas.

"Handle the bill bro," I said to him, "I'll get up with you later."

He took the money, but the look on his face remained the same. There was more to the story. I could feel it, and it put a sour taste in my mouth. *Maybe Sundai was used goods. How could a woman like that bust it open for a random stranger at an airport? Had she busted it open? What the hell happened? What the hell is Lucas talking about?* Thoughts ran through my mind at a hundred miles per hour as we waited for the valet to bring my car to the front of the restaurant. I glanced over at Sundai. A lone tear slid down her cheek, her breathing was sporadic, and she was damn near shaking. I didn't know the backstory, but whatever it was had her visually shaken up. Before I could ask her what was wrong or offer an ounce of comfort, the valet attendant pulled my Infiniti QX56 up towards the entrance. The radio was thumping, and one scowl from me encouraged the young kid to dial the volume down. I knew how much beat was in the truck, it was my play car. I had an old Toyota Tundra that I drove back and forth to work, but my Infiniti was my baby.

I opened Sundai's door, and she slid into the car without a word. I didn't push anything. I felt like she would open up and tell me whenever she wanted to. The drive back to my street was quiet, and I almost felt like she was avoiding eye contact and conversation on purpose. She stared out of the window or at her phone like either was more interesting than me. I was slightly confused and slightly offended. I didn't know what I had done to make her so standoffish, but I didn't like it at all.

I pulled up on the street and threw caution to the wind. I guess the familiarity gave me courage, or maybe it was the drink from Chill. Either way, I was feeling froggish and about to leap.

"So, would you like to come over to my place and kick it for a bit?" I asked Sundai.

She hesitated and I studied her face for a reaction. I could see the apprehension written all over her face. It only added to my confusion, though. It was eating away at me, but I was intent on not pressuring the answer out of her.

"Why?" She rebutted, "You heard what your brother said."

That was it—that was the straw that broke the camel's back for me.

"Yes, I heard him. What did he mean?"

"He came onto me at the airport," she admitted.

My breathing quickened and I could feel my heart skipping a few beats. I was so enthralled with her that I had no clue of what I would do if she blurted out an answer that I didn't like. Her fucking around with my brother was so unexpected that I choked on the air I was inhaling.

"He came on to you?" I repeated as she turned in her seat to face me and nodded her head in response.

"Did you guys—you know?"

"No, we did not!"

That is all I needed to hear. I exhaled the breath I had been holding. I don't know what it was about Sundai, but I believed her.

"Cool," I said, "If you say you didn't, I believe you. Besides, if you did you had no way of knowing he was my brother. Everything is okay, I promise you."

It seemed like a weight was lifted from her shoulders as a smile eased across her face. It made me feel better, and the air inside of the car was lighter.

"Come over," I reiterated, "just for a few. I know that you have things to do."

"Alright."

CHAPTER 14

Lucas

I was irritated as hell that my brother chose to chase a skirt instead of hanging with me. It was supposed to be bros over hoes. Hell, it was supposed to be bros over everything. I guess Bryce's focus had changed a little bit, and I didn't like it at all. I scowled at his back as he exited Chill. I thought about chasing after him, but I quickly decided against it. This was not a fight I would win in this public place, but I would make it my business to let him know how I felt once we were alone. He was the older brother, but I didn't give a shit. Wrong was wrong, and in my mind he definitely was wrong.

"Can I get a dessert?" Alaisha spoke up.

I hunched my shoulders, and I honestly didn't care. Bryce left more than enough money, so whatever she ordered would be on him. She waved the server over and ordered a serving of beignets.

"Would you like the chocolate sauce or the caramel sauce?" Mari asked.

"Chocolate please."

Alaisha's eyes met mine, and the unspoken thoughts she had were loud and clear to me. Maybe the thoughts came from my own filthy mind. I didn't know or care, but I was going to bring them into fruition.

"Mari, make that two," I spoke up, "I'll take mine to go with an extra sauce, please."

She nodded her head and turned to fulfill our order. I waited patiently until the order was filled and delivered to our table. I took in the ambience of the entire restaurant. I have to admit, it was nice, and I felt like Sundai was lucky. Bryce definitely pulled out all of the stops to impress her and I wondered if she was even worth it.

Thirty minutes later, I was walking into my hotel suite with my beignets tucked under my arm and Alaisha on my heels. She came right in and headed straight for the shower. She moved around my room like she owned it. It was like she had permission, and she hadn't asked for it. I wondered if she felt like the pussy she was throwing had that much power. It really didn't, but if she was handing it out for free, I would definitely take full advantage of it. I would dick her down and kick her out without batting an eyelash. I wasn't sure what was on her agenda, but sex was the only thing on mine. I hoped she didn't feel too attached or led on by me asking her to go to Chill with me. There weren't any romantic sentiments involved. I'd leave the wining and dining to Bryce—I wasn't the type.

When the water turned off in the bathroom, I was naked and stretched out across the king-sized bed. My legs were spread open, and my manhood hung wherever it wanted to. I scanned the length of her body. She was dressed in a pale pink thong and bra set that she could have kept. I didn't care. My little man did though because it started throbbing as soon as I saw her. He was such a man-whore. It was like a pussy detector. It knew when it was about to get some, and I never could deprive him. It wasn't in my nature.

"Is that for me?" She said as she pointed at my semi-hard erection.

"Soon," I admitted, "Lie down, and pull that fake ass Victoria Secret off."

She looked like I hurt her feelings, but she peeled off both pieces of underwear before crawling onto the bed. She grasped for the duvet in a frail attempt to cover her nakedness. My strength overcame hers as I snatched the covers from her and tossed them to the floor.

"Stop playing," I growled, "you know what time it is."

She stopped trying to fight instantaneously and watched me intently to see what my next move was going to be. I eased my way across the room to the Chill bag. I removed the chocolate syrup and the extra container from the bag before returning to where she lay waiting patiently for the smack down that was coming.

I wasn't a super affectionate person. In fact, I wasn't affectionate at all anymore thanks to Keili Chevan Gregory. She was my kryptonite, and she knew it. She managed to run off with another man, and when she did, she snatched my heart from my chest and stomped all over it. A sour taste formed in my mouth as I thought about Keili, but I swallowed hard and refocused on the task at hand. There was a beautiful woman lying in my bed. I had been curious about what she tasted like from the moment our eyes connected, so I decided to indulge in her for a little while.

I poured the chocolate syrup down the center of her chest and abdomen. She giggled as the lukewarm liquid contacted her skin.

"Oh, you're nasty nasty, huh?"

I didn't want to tell her to shut the fuck up, but the words were dancing at the tip of my tongue. I knew that my curtness would ruin the mood. She was sadly mistaken if she felt like what was going on was for her benefit. It was, but it was for mine as well. She had been a hankering desire in my mind. My mouth watered like a crack fiend whenever she was around, but I willed myself to keep my mouth to myself until this very moment. I knew what kind of skills I possessed, and it was the kind that damaged women. I had the type of tongue that turned innocent women into stalkers. It's the kind of tongue that had bitches waiting outside of my job or hiding in the bushes outside of my apartment. I hoped that Alaisha wouldn't become as needy when I was done with her. I sent up a quick prayer as I watched the chocolate sauce trickle down her chest. The sight sent an insatiable fire to my manhood, and I felt the blood rushing in that direction.

I closed the space between us until I was face-to-face with her breasts. They were at least a C-cup, and I loved that shit. They were big enough to jiggle in her sundress, but they were still perky, and her nipples were rock-hard. I admired her shape as I took my tongue and cuffed it around the right nipple. She instantly arched her back away from the bed. The hisses and moans she made didn't distract me from the task at hand. I licked and slurped all of the chocolate from her chest and moved lower and lower until I was face to face with her navel. I stuck my tongue in it for the hell of it before moving to her juicy center.

"What the hell," she said as she tried to close her legs around my head. I wasn't having that at all, though. I used what seemed like all of my upper body strength to pry her legs open and hold them there as I unleashed an assault on her clit. The motion of my tongue sent a series of chills over her body, and I relished in the moment. The sweet taste of her sex mixed with the chocolate on my tongue was intoxicating.

"Oooh daddy," she moaned as she gyrated her hips against my face, "I'm ready for that dick."

The pool of moisture that had accumulated at her center was a key indicator of how turned on she was, but I wasn't there yet. My tongue needed attention, and then I would handle my dick. Her body tensed, and I knew that she was on the brink of having her first orgasm. I sucked her soul through her vagina before I moved on to my next escapade. Her eyes clenched tight as she came, and her body jerked violently. It reminded me of how Keili's body reacted when I tongue kissed her vagina. Memories flooded my mind of the woman I thought I would give my all to. She was the woman that I saw myself spending the rest of forever with and the woman that I thought would bear my kids. Anger flooded my body and threatened to overcome the ecstasy that I felt at that moment.

"Turn over," I barked at Alaisha.

She did so with no complaints or rebuttals. I grasped at her hips until her back was bent into the perfect arch. The position brought me face-to-face with her round ass. I was satisfied because it distracted me from the love faces that she made and any thoughts of Keili that tried to invade the moment I was having with Alaisha. The pain Keili caused was still fresh. Every day, I tried to put a band-aid over it and move on, but it was not working.

Thoughts of Keili caused a sour taste to form in my mouth. I tried to swallow it down, but I was unsuccessful. Instead, I hawked and spit a glob of saliva right onto Alaisha's backside. I watched intently as the spit rolled down the crack of her ass. The sight turned me on even more. I held my manhood in place as what was left coated the head and skin of my dick. I knew what was coming next, and a part of me wondered if she did. A bigger part of me didn't give a fuck. She knew what she was getting into when she came back to this room.

I forcefully rammed my dick into her ass. I felt her body tense beneath me. She let out an exasperated sigh as she tried to get away from me. My hands on her hips held her tightly in place as I carelessly slid in and out of her ass. I didn't care that she may not have been used to someone as girthy as me tapping at her back door. I disregarded the tears that fell freely from her face. I pounded her ass like there was no tomorrow. All of the pain Keili caused resurfaced. I could visualize her telling me that the child she was pregnant with was not mine, and I drilled Alaisha harder. The day Keili left was a vivid memory in my mind. The way she and my best friend, Milo, played in my face and laughed as they pulled off was a rerun that I wanted to stop playing. The pain I felt was evident in my strokes. They were hard, reckless, and full of malice. Somewhere in the distance I heard Alaisha scream. It wasn't a pleasurable scream. Instead, it was one filled with pain and even fear. She sounded like a wounded animal, but I didn't stop. I couldn't stop. I wouldn't stop until Keili felt all of the wrath in my head. I would make her hurt as much as I was hurting.

After what felt like hours, I felt my orgasm building. I ejaculated on Alaisha's ass and back before she collapsed flat on the bed. She was still and lifeless, but her sobs filled the silent room around us.

"You, okay?" I managed to say.

She jerked her head around to face me. Her eyes were blood-shot red, and the makeup she had worn to Chill was ruined.

"What do you think?" She asked between sobs, "What the fuck is wrong with you?"

When I didn't offer an answer right away, she stumbled out of bed and began to get dressed. I knew she was about to leave, and I did absolutely nothing to stop her. She had finally gotten the hint I had been giving. She was sex to me—nothing more, nothing less. I took a seat at the desk that was positioned on one side of the room and watched as she picked up the last of her stuff and headed towards the door. She glanced back in my direction as she reached for the handle. I didn't offer any of the commiserations that she was looking for, so she slid out of the door without another word to me.

CHAPTER 15
Sundai

W e hopped out of Bryce's car and made the short walk across the lawn to his front door.

I stood patiently as he inserted his key and pushed the chocolate-colored door open. A part of me expected to see a typical bachelor pad. I just knew the house would contain a television, mix matched furniture, and little to no decorum otherwise. I felt like it would lack sophistication, but I was pleasantly surprised. The black leather sofa drew my attention to the center of the living room, but it was easily paired with an abstract black and grey rug. The room was littered with art and more surprisingly—books.

"You're a reader?" I asked as he stepped into the space.

He motioned for me to have a seat on the sofa, and I obliged. He sat a few inches away from me. He sat close enough for it to be personal, but not close enough to make it awkward or overbearing.

"Believe it or not, I'm an avid reader and trivia buff," he said, answering my question.

I was pleasantly surprised. I loved reading as well, and it made me happy to know that we had that in common.

"What's your favorite genre? Favorite author?" I asked. I didn't believe him one bit, so I was putting him on the spot. At least, I thought I was.

"I'll read almost anything, but I especially love romance and urban fiction novels," he started, "my favorite authors are Zoe Ray, Khatari, and R. Coxton."

I hadn't heard of any of the authors he mentioned, so I made a mental note to check them out later. I was just thrilled to find someone who operated the way I did. I watched intently as he poured himself a drink. He offered one to me, but I quickly declined. The alcohol from Chill was enough. The last thing I wanted to do was be somewhere face down and ass up in this man's house. Deep inside, I would not mind it. I was deeply attracted to him. I had been since the moment he waltzed across the yard and into my life. It was something about his body that seemed to call out to mine, and she wanted to answer. He took his seat on the couch next to me, and I was noticing things about him that I hadn't noticed about him before. My eyes took inventory of every inch of his body that I could place my lips on. I imagined leaving my lip gloss prints all over his Hershey chocolate skin.

"Sundai, did you hear me?" He asked.

I readjusted my focus, slightly embarrassed that I hadn't heard anything he said. I shook the lustful thoughts from my head and tried to focus on the conversation instead.

"Sorry, what did you say?"

"I was asking about Ms. Opal's services," he said.

"Oh. Everything was pretty easy. I just have to go up to the funeral home one day this week. I'm aiming for one day this weekend."

He nodded his head in understanding as sadness washed over his face. He was visibly torn up, and it broke my heart. Over the past few months, he had developed a relationship with my mother in my absence. It made my heart swell to know that someone was here with her, but it hurt me to my core to know that he was grieving as well. I saw a tear glisten against his skin, and I took the opportunity to swipe it away before he could react. The moment my hand caressed his face, it was like an electric current surged through both of us.

He closed the space between us until I could feel his sporadic breathing on my lips. My heartbeat quickened, and I wondered if he was going to kiss me or pull away. I felt like he was going to pull back in any second, so I took it upon myself to remove any chance he had of reneging. I quickly flattened my lips against his and relished in the moment. He parted his lips and invited my tongue to intertwine with his. I didn't shy away. Instead, I slithered my tongue into his mouth. The taste of liquor was fresh on his tongue, and it worked like gasoline to my fire. I moaned softly as he reached around my waist and rested his hand in the small of my back. A sensual rush overcame me, and I melted into his arms. The air around us seemed heavy, and I struggled to breathe. The temperature in the house went from pleasant to a few degrees past hell. The only thought on my mind was getting naked and doing something very inappropriate in his living room. It had been a little over a year since I had sex with anyone, and the lady downstairs was crying out loud and clear. I could hear her, and it seemed like my pulse was drumming in my ears as I kissed him. I had heard people speak of seeing fireworks as they kissed someone. However, I never had the pleasure of experiencing it until I kissed Bryce.

His hands explored more of my body, and they seemed to set fever to whatever part he touched. It felt good but wrong at the same time. I melted like hot butter in his arms, and he was there to spread me over a hot biscuit. Just the thought of a biscuit opened the floodgates, and all of the memories of my mom flooded my mind. The reason for me coming home stood front and center in my mind, and anything else all of a sudden felt irrelevant. I didn't disconnect our lips right away. I didn't want to interrupt the electricity that was coursing through me. I felt selfish. Here I was fighting a mental battle, on the verge of a breakdown, and I refused to stop kissing this man.

The tears flowed warmly against my skin and mixed with our kisses. I felt bad for crying, but I really couldn't help it. My emotional levees burst wide open, and there wasn't any repairing them. Everything hit me like a ton of bricks, and it hit me all at once.

"Damn," Bryce said as he broke our kiss, "I didn't think I was that bad of a kisser."

I managed to squeeze out a giggle.

"The kiss was marvelous. It just shouldn't have happened. I shouldn't be here."

I jumped up from my place on the couch and started back pedaling towards the door. He sat with his glass clutched in his hand and a look on his face that instantly made me feel bad. He looked like someone had snatched the last Oreo cookie out of his pack. He had been eating them, they had gotten good to him, and someone snatched his last one and took the fuck off. As bad as I felt, it didn't stop me from running out of his door and towards my mother's house. I didn't look back, and my feet didn't stop.

A few days passed, and I managed to push any impure thoughts about Bryce to the back of my mind. I saw him passing a few times, he waved, and I kept moving. I had enough on my mind when it came to planning a nice homecoming for my mom. A few trips to the funeral home, and I was exhausted with the entire process. I needed a distraction, but I knew that Bryce was out of the question. He needed to be anyway.

The morning of the funeral arrived, and my attitude was somber. The form fitting little black dress and fishnet stockings I wore left little to nothing to the imagination. The wide brim black hat with the mini veil in the front and the dark sunglasses I wore worked to cover the emotions that were written all over my face. I was sure my eyes were puffy and a weird shade of red that didn't match my ensemble. It was a key indicator of the mood that I was in and the fact that I didn't manage to get any sleep the night before. I had been going back and forth to the funeral home, but nothing cemented the fact that I had lost my mother until I saw her lying in her powder pink casket. The white skirt suit I picked out for her was a nice contrast to the pink velvet interior of the casket. She looked nice, and the slight smile on her face made me feel like she was at peace. I was glad for that much because I was not.

CHAPTER 16

Bryce

I was appreciative of the fact that Ms. Opal's funeral arrangements were shared in the local newspaper. I wanted to attend and pay my respects, but I hadn't spoken to Sundai since she sat in my living room. That fact alone confused me. I thought everything was going so well. We were both adults, and we went for what we wanted. I thought everything was going well until I tasted the saltiness of her tears. Not only was she crying, but she jumped up and ran out without explaining why. The man in me wanted to comfort her and make sure she was okay, but I decided to just give her space. Maybe she would come back around soon. I prayed that she would.

After the funeral, cars gathered next door for what I assumed to be a repast or visitation of some sort. I quickly changed out of my dress clothes and replaced them with a t-shirt, jogging pants, and Nike slide shoes. I walked across the lawn heading straight for Ms. Opal's door. Two elderly ladies that I had never seen sat on the porch.

"Well, hello," One of them spoke to me as I approached.

"Hello."

"You must be Bryce. Opal was always talking about the handsome young man that lived next door to her."

"Yes, I am," I confirmed, "but I'm a disadvantage because I don't know who you are."

"I'm Estelle and this is Edna," the lady introduced, "We played bingo with Opal at the senior center."

I nodded my head in understanding. Opal caught the bus to the senior center twice a week. She always joked that the building was musty and the people who went were too old for her. It made me smile to see them supporting her, even in death.

"Mrs. Estelle, don't be out here harassing Bryce," Sundai said as she came to the door with a plate of pound cake for each of them.

"Honey, someone needs to harass this young man, and it ain't me," she said as she winked in Sundai's direction.

I struggled to stifle a laugh as Sundai looked back and forth from the little, frail lady to me.

"Bryce, thank you for coming to the funeral," Sundai said, finally focusing her attention solely on me.

"I wouldn't be anywhere else."

It came out a little stronger than I would have liked it too, but it was the truth. There wasn't any other I would have been. A part of me was there to support her and an even bigger part of me was there for Ms. Opal. She was like a second mother to me so not attending her funeral would be blasphemous. Our eyes locked for a brief moment, and the emotion behind them was unreadable. Hurt and sadness was evident, but there was something else that I couldn't quite recognize. It awakened something deep inside of me, and I wanted to take her somewhere private and do some very private things to her. Our kiss was still fresh on my mind even though I tried to forget about it. We held on to the stare a few minutes longer than necessary, and it was only broken when one of the women on the porch cleared her throat.

"Bryce, would you like something to eat?" Sundai asked awkwardly.

I nodded my head and followed her through the crowded house to the kitchen where some older women were putting the food into Tupperware containers for later.

"Sorry y'all," Sundai said politely, "Bryce needs a plate."

"Not a problem, darling. We will fix him one," she said, "Is there anything you do not eat?"

"No ma'am, but can you make it to go?"

I stood to the side as their gloved hands went to work placing ham, fried chicken, beans, and other commodities on my plate. I couldn't help stealing glances at Sundai. Even in mourning, she was the most beautiful woman I had ever met. She didn't even know it, but I was smitten with her. I would move heaven and hell for her, and she had no idea whatsoever. All she did was stand there in all of her natural, hypnotizing beauty. She was everything and more, and I needed her. Something about her drew me into her space. She was the sun of my life, and I would be happy to spend my life orbiting in her space. I was never a believer in love at first sight, but Ms. Opal was right. She knew that I would love Sundai.

"Here you go young man," one of the women said to me as she handed me a healthy, heavy plateful of food.

"So, I've been meaning to ask you something," Sundai said to me as we meandered through the crowd of people.

"Anything." I said as my heart quickened as I waited to hear what she had to say.

"So, I'll be going home soon. I'm going to have to take Kane somewhere. Opal would resurrect and kill me if he got put down. Y'all seem to be really cozy, so I wanted to see if you would take him."

I laughed out loud. Out of all the things she could ask, I was not expecting that to be the question. I hadn't had a pet since I moved into my house, and I didn't plan on getting one. The look on her face was so sexy and sincere. I would've adopted Cujo if she had asked me to.

"I think mom would like it this way," she spoke again before I had the chance to respond.

The thought of Ms. Opal smiling down on me and her over-grown baby of a dog instantly made me smile. He seemed like a good dog, and he could guard the house while I was at work. It would give me some company and another reason to see Sundai, so I shrugged my shoulders.

"I guess I could," I said to her, "it couldn't be that bad."

"If you say so, that dog doesn't heel for anybody except Opal."

"So, when are you leaving us?" I asked her, waiting for the bomb to drop.

"Soon. I was going to wait around to get the house sold, but I changed my mind. I just need to get away from here and clear my mind," she said.

I couldn't help but think that when she said the words 'clear my mind,' she wasn't just talking about the funeral. She was also talking about me.

CHAPTER 17

Alaisha

I sat in my office and let my mind wander wherever it pleased. It always found a way back to Lucas, and that alone repulsed me. It was a slow day at the hotel. It was already after noon, and we had only had one check-in which was ludicrous for our brand on a Saturday afternoon.

The phone rang interrupting any thoughts I could have had. It was the front desk clerk, Kendra. She informed me that she would be setting out lunch soon, and she asked if I wanted anything. I loved working for this particular hotel. We were one of the only ones in the world that served our patrons a hot breakfast as well as a hot lunch. The lunch consisted of random flavored paninis, potato chips, fruit, and sometimes a hot soup depending on how she felt. It was a small variety of items, but it was lunch, nonetheless. I knew our patrons appreciated it as I appreciated it on days that I didn't feel like going out to grab something.

"What's on the menu today?" I asked into the receiver.

"Hot ham and cheese sandwiches, meatball sliders, chips, a melon mixture and chicken and rice soup," she said.

I loved it when I worked alongside Kendra. She was a professionally trained chef, and as long as I kept the kitchen stocked, she blessed us with delicious courses.

"I'll bring you up something," she added.

"Actually, I'll come down and get it."

We disconnected the call, and my mind wandered back to Lucas. We hadn't spoken since the stunt he pulled in his room, and I felt thwarted. I felt like he owed me some type of explanation. What type of man violently fucks a woman in her ass and sits silently as she runs out of the door. Red flags should have been screaming at me. I knew it. I should have packed my shit, left his room, and never looked back in his direction. God had given me a way out, and I was playing the dumb damsel that kept putting herself in harm's way. He was predatorial in the way that he handled me, and the retarded rabbit kept right back hopping into the wolves' den. I shook my head incessantly. I knew I was being foolish, but I couldn't help but think that this man had some hidden layers that he wasn't showing. His tongue between my thighs was sensual, soft even. So, I know that he had that side of himself. That was the side I wanted to bring to the forefront. He was like an onion to me, and I wanted to peel back his many layers. I didn't care if I shed a few tears along the way.

I hadn't seen him around the hotel since I left his room, so I really didn't even know if he was still there. He could've packed up and headed to parts unknown for all I knew. I could've been sitting in my office pondering over a man that had hauled ass days ago. There was only one way for me to be sure. I typed his room number into our computer system. I knew that I couldn't search via name. I only knew his first name—Lucas. I could remember his room number like it was embedded in my brain. I typed it in, and to my surprise he was still there. Not only was he still in the hotel, but he extended his stay.

My heart fluttered a little when I saw that his name was still registered as a guest at our hotel. I grabbed my lip gloss, refreshed my lips, and headed downstairs to the lunch buffet area. I grabbed a ham and cheese sandwich, a bowl of soup, and some fruit and made my way to a table by the window. The table allowed me to see the beautiful weather outside of the window, but it also gave me a full vantage point of the dining room and front door of the hotel. The dining room was completely empty except for me and Kendra who kept checking and refreshing the food. I was four bites into my sandwich before the elevator dinged alerting me that someone was coming down to grab a bite to eat. I secretly wished for it to be Lucas. Instead, a muscular white man wearing a sleeveless shirt that read "Gym Shark" and a matching pair of shorts wandered into the lobby. I took notice of everything about him. The cool shade of blue of his eyes reminded me of the two pools that we had on the roof. He grabbed a bowl of fruit and something to drink before returning to the elevator. He pressed the button, calling the elevator to the lobby. When the silvery doors slid open the man halted allowing who ever was inside to step off. I damn near choked on a piece of cantaloupe when I saw who it was. His all-black jogging pants and black fitted t-shirt left nothing unillustrated. The tee was fitted and hung to every muscle in his biceps, pecs, and abdominal muscles. I imagined that he didn't have on any underwear under his jogging pants because I recognized the print of the monster between his legs instantly. Maybe, it was my own feverish imagination, but I knew the thang between his legs was definitely thanging, hanging, and swanging.

He surveyed the dining room before moving to fix a plate of his own. He hadn't even acknowledged me sitting there, and I knew he saw me. Hell, I was the only person sitting there. Besides, the romper I wore from Fashion Nova turned heads wherever I went. It was burnt orange with a plunging neckline. My girls were nice and perky, and my face card rarely declined. He grabbed whatever he wanted and took a seat at a table a few feet away from where I was sitting. He didn't speak, but instead proceeded to eat his lunch like I wasn't even there. He carried himself like I was not worthy enough to breathe his air and it irritated the hell out of me. I grabbed my things and took a seat across from him at his table. He paused from eating to stare at me like I had lost my damn mind.

"What are you doing Alaisha?" He asked.

"Oh, so you do see me?"

"I saw you when I walked in here, but I really just want to eat my lunch. Take whatever BS you're on back over there," he said pointing at my original table.

"No BS," I conceded, "I just have a question."

He exhaled sharply but refused to remove his gaze from me. His stare was icy and unwelcoming. It caused me to fidget in my seat a little, but I refused to back down from him. He was not the big, bad wolf—not this time.

"What the hell happened the other night?" I asked.

I didn't even look around to see who may have overheard our conversation. Kendra could have been right there eavesdropping on what she would consider to be "juicy tea" to run back and spill with the other employees. At that point, I didn't care. I just needed the answer to my question. I needed closure.

"I fucked you and sent you on your way," he answered nonchalantly, "What else is there to talk about?"

"I never imagined you to be so cruel and coldhearted."

"You don't know me."

"Why can't I get to know you?"

"I'm not here for that. Love is for the weak. A bitch will smile in your face all while fucking your best friend. I'll be damned if I go out like a sucker again."

CHAPTER 18

Lucas

I just wanted to go downstairs and eat a quick lunch. I had been cooped up in my room, so it was a nice change of scenery. I prayed that I didn't run into Alaisha's ass. I mean, it would be a blessing in disguise if I got a chance to slide between her thighs again. She was on some lovey dovey shit, and I wasn't trying to go there with her. I hadn't loved another woman since Keili, and I didn't intend to lower my guard anytime soon. I knew it was a defense mechanism, but I found it easier to fuck them and leave them.

I stepped off the elevator and the bright lobby caught me off-guard. I had the blackout curtains closed in my room and rarely turned on any lights. The darkness relaxed me, so the contrasting brightness of the lobby surprised me. I looked around briefly as I grabbed a plate. I noticed her. I saw her the moment I stepped off of the elevator. I couldn't help but see her. She was absolutely radiant in her outfit of choice. In another lifetime, I would be glad to wife her. I'd take her off the market and fill her with my babies so quickly it would make her head spin. She was a baddie to say the least. Her body was thick and curvy, and her face was that of a model.

I sat down at the table of my choosing, but I could feel her eyes stalking me the entire time. I didn't say anything to her, and she didn't say anything either. The tension was thicker than she was. I knew that something was about to happen, so I sat down and braced myself for it.

Sure enough, she completely uprooted from her table to come confront me at mine. The issue at hand was me not saying anything, and I found myself wanting to be completely honest with her.

"Why can't I get to know you?"

"I'm not here for that. Love is for the weak. A bitch will smile in your face all while fucking your best friend. I'll be damned if I go out like a sucker again."

"I'm not that woman," she said as she stared directly in my face, "the woman that would hurt you."

I let out an exasperated humph as I bit into my sandwich. In all honesty, I wasn't up for this discussion with her, but something about her tenacity seemed to turn me on. It was something about the way she grabbed the bull by the horns and went after what she wanted that made me feel some type of way. I wanted to stop talking, eating, and interrupt any other plans she may have had for the rest of the day. I just wanted her face down and ass up in my hotel room.

"Stop looking at me like that," she said, interrupting my thoughts and bringing my naughty mind back to her conversation.

"Like what?"

"Like I'm a prime rib slathered in gravy," she said with a laugh that resonated to parts of my body that it shouldn't have.

"I like prime rib, and I'll suck the gravy off of you."

A slight blush spread across her face, and for a moment I thought I had her tangled in my crosshairs. A slight shake of her head, and she was back on the same bullshit she was on when she moved to my table.

"I'm not doing this with you," she announced, "You can't just fuck me and toss me to the side whenever you want."

"Why not?"

"*Why not?* Because I'm not a toy. I am a woman with feelings," she said to me, and I smirked in response.

"You know what, Lucas? Fuck you." She spat at me, but it didn't hurt my feelings at all.

"Finally, we're on the same page. You know where to find me when you're ready," I said before rising from the table, leaving her sitting there with her mouth hanging open.

I rocked up instantly at the thought of me sliding in and out of her open mouth. I felt like I had a good read on the situation, and I knew it was only going to be a matter of time before she abandoned her lunch and followed me upstairs. I planted a seed, and I knew that it would grow.

I hopped on the elevator and went right to my room. I wasted no time getting completely naked. I counted the minutes in my head. Seven went by before I heard a light tap on the door. Before I could get up to open the door, the lock clicked, and the door swung open. I was tickled to see that she had the keycard to my room. The wishy-washy bullshit was killing me softly. There was no denying that she wanted what she was about to get.

CHAPTER 19
Alaisha

Lucas' cocky ass attitude irked me to my core. It was like he knew what he did got under my skin. He knew what buttons to push and how hard to push them. I sat at the table and watched his back until the elevator doors closed. I wrestled with my thoughts—to go or not to go was the question. Red flags popped up whenever I thought about him and his behavior. I didn't even know his full name, but as far as I was concerned it could have been Lucas Red Flag. He was toxic in every sense of the word, but for some reason I couldn't stay away from him. When he walked into the room and his scent hit my nostril it released pheromones that I hadn't planned on. My nipples got rock hard in my romper, and I could feel the moisture pooling between my legs. I tried hard to put up a front like I wasn't bothered by him.

My mind wrestled with my body as I sat at his table surrounded by the remnants of whatever cologne he chose to wear. Finally, my body won. I went to the front desk, created an extra key card, and was on my way upstairs. For any other guest, they might find my actions offensive, but I knew that Lucas wouldn't care. He bated me really well, and I was about to let him reel me in—again.

I slid the keycard into its reader and let the door swing open. The light from the hallway engulfed the darkness in his room, and it cast the perfect spotlight on his naked body. I knew he was with the shits, but I never expected him to be in his birthday suit by the time I made it upstairs. I hesitated for a moment as I let the door close behind me.

"So, what's the move?" he asked rather impatiently.

I peeled the romper I was wearing off and left it by the door. I took a few steps before I peeled out of the thong and bra I was wearing underneath. I was completely nude like Lucas, but I froze in place. I wanted him, but my feet wouldn't let me take another step towards the bed.

"If I have to come over there and get you, you aren't going to like it," he threatened.

"Lucas."

"Alaisha."

"I want more than this. I deserve more than this," I said in a voice barely audible.

He sat up on the side of the bed and slid his feet into shoes. It was dark in the room, and it took a few minutes for my eyes to adjust. I studied his shadowy figure as he sat on the edge of the bed. A part of me knew that he was about to hold true to his threat and come and get me. I braced myself for whatever was about to take place.

"I don't know if I can give you more than this," he admitted, "Why are you stuck on me anyway? All the men you come across, and you're stuck on one that doesn't want to be stuck."

His words stung to my core and caused me to backtrack towards the clothes I had dropped. The silk of my underwear tickled my ankles, and I reached down and grabbed both pieces and began putting them back on.

"You leaving?" he asked, "I thought—"

"Yea, well I thought you were a better man than you turned out to be."

I slid my romper back on effortlessly and eased out of the door. Hot tears stung as they rolled down my cheek, but I refused to give him anymore of myself. I tucked my feelings, my pride, and everything else and strutted down the hall towards my office. I passed the sideways glance and raised eyebrow of Kendra.

"Girl, where'd you dip off too so quick?" she asked nosily.

I cocked my head to the side as I contemplated the nicest way to tell her to mind her own damned business.

"I saw you sitting there with that fine specimen of a man. I went to check the soup, and when I looked around again both of you were gone. I just know y'all didn't leave together," she said with a wink and a smile that only irritated me more.

I rolled my eyes and kept walking. I didn't stop until I reached the comfort of my office. The oversized, white leather chair called to me, and I didn't hesitate to plop down in it. The events of the past few minutes played in my head like a bad movie that I couldn't turn off, or a horrible book that I refused to put down until I finished it.

Lucas's words echoed in my mind loud and clear. *All the men you come across, and you're stuck on one that doesn't want to be stuck.* He was right, and I couldn't quite put my finger on what magnetized me to him. I was obviously attracted to him, and I felt like he needed saving. I could be the superwoman to defrost his heart, if only he would let me. I didn't know what made him think that he was not worthy of love, and I didn't know what made me even give a damn. The way he acted toward me should've been enough to make me run away and not look back but instead, my heart ached for him. I wanted to show him the pleasant side of love. I wanted to make him happy.

CHAPTER 20

Bryce

The first few days with my new pet went off without a hitch. He had to get used to my personality, and I had to get used to his. Sundai was right, Ms. Opal had him spoiled rotten. I sat in my recliner after work one evening, and he started to whine profusely. He started to sniff the living room and prance around in circles.

"You better not use the bathroom in here," I said to him.

As soon as he heard the word bathroom, he went into what could only be considered as hyper mode.

"Alright. Alright," I said as I jumped up to grab his leash and attach it to his collar.

We headed towards the door, and I prayed that we made it out of it before he had an accident. I was tired, and cleaning up behind this dog was not on the agenda. After a brisk walk around the neighborhood, I noticed Sundai loading some items into her car. As if he could sense my thoughts, Kane headed straight in her direction.

"Hey, Kane baby," She said as she bent down to rub his waiting head, "Hello, Bryce."

"Hi, Sundai. Do you need any help?"

"No, thank you. I'm about done."

She stuffed the last purple suitcase into the backseat of the car before turning back in our direction. Her eyes met mine, and a twinge of possessiveness surged through me. I knew that she would be heading home one day, but I silently wished that she would do so in the dead of night. I didn't want to have to watch her leave.

"You heading home?" I asked like I didn't know the answer already.

"Yep. Gotta get back to work," she said.

"When are you leaving?"

"The first flight out of here. Probably tomorrow morning," she said, and it felt like my heart dropped down to my stomach.

"How about the second flight out of here?"

"Excuse me?"

"Can I take you on a date before you leave? I mean a real one. We need a do over from the catastrophe with me brother."

"I don't know," she answered hesitantly.

"Just one date. No strings attached or anything. Then, you can fly back to your fancy smancy news and forget all about us down here in the country."

I said it jokingly, but I hope she felt the shade I was throwing. Hell, at this point, I uprooted an entire tree and chunked it at her. That's exactly what I predicted would happen. She would go back to life as normal, and I would never lay eyes on her beautiful face again. I mean, I guess I could watch her on the news, but was it really the same? Kane stroked his head against the outside of her thigh, and the whine that accompanied it tickled me. It was almost as if he was encouraging her to say yes to a date with me.

"How can I say no?" was all she said.

I smiled as the wheels started to turn in my head. I watched her walk inside of her mother's house before me and Kane retired to ours. I had some things I needed to handle.

CHAPTER 21

Bryce

A light jog across the grass, and Kane and I were home. He seemed tired from the walk that I thought was light-work. He found his bed, and I found my recliner. I was filled with nervous energy. I felt like a child anticipating Christmas, and I knew it was all because of Sundai. I felt like I needed another opportunity to prove that I wasn't the guy she thought I was. I needed to show her that I wasn't Lucas.

I sat in my recliner, and my brother crossed my mind. I hadn't seen him since I walked out of Chill with Sundai. He was seething, and I knew it. It was always about him. Even when it wasn't about him, he found some kind of twisted self-centered way to make it about him. I shook my head as I thought about his behavior. Almost as if my thoughts manifested him, my phone rang.

"Yo."

"What's up, Bro" he asked, "I see you finally got your head outta Sundai's ass."

Sundai's name rolling off his lips instantly irritated the shit out of me. I didn't know what his angle was, but I did know that she didn't deserve to be a part of it. I instantly wanted him off my phone. I knew that he had come into town to see me, but at this point it didn't matter. His birthday was approaching, and I didn't want it spoiled on my behalf.

"You know a nigga birthday is tomorrow," he spoke as if he had read my mind again.

I inhaled deeply and focused on being cordial before I spoke again.

"Oh yea. What are you going to do for it?"

"I was hoping we could pop a couple of brews and put something good on the grill like we used to do back in the day. Just me and you."

I knew what the last part of his sentence was insinuating without him having to go into specifics, but I decided to push my luck anyway.

"You sure you don't want a party? I can invite Sundai, and you can bring that lil' lady you brough to Chill."

"I'm no longer seeing that lil' lady," he said in a tone that made me think twice about asking questions.

Lucas was my brother, and I knew how he was. I knew all about what happened between him and his ex-fiancé. I also knew that it froze what was left of his heart. Seeing him at Chill with a woman gave me an ounce of hope, but he easily diminished any hope I had of seeing him with a woman. It wasn't like I didn't know what happened. A part of me hated the hell out of Keili for what she did. He had given all of himself to her, and she had run off on the plug like she didn't give a damn. In reality, she deserved whatever was coming her way. I often wondered what type of woman led a man on only to break him down and crush his spirit. Lucas wasn't always the cold-hearted, demon of a man that he is now. He actually cared with his heart and not his throbbing manhood. We were raised by the same person, so I knew that his standards mirrored my own.

I made up my mind that I would take Sundai out that morning or early afternoon, which would leave her plenty of time to catch a flight to wherever she wanted to go. My heart stung whenever I thought about her leaving. I had just met her, but her mother made it seem like I had known her my entire life. I felt like she was the missing piece of my soul or my rib. I used my phone to order a few things from the local grocery store. I would have them delivered early the next morning. I felt satisfied because my plan was slowly coming into fruition. I didn't know if she was a picnic kind of girl. She may have been the kind that hated the outdoors. You know, the kind who hated bugs, dirt, and sunlight. I was never the type to go hike on a mountain, but I did enjoy being outside soaking up the sun. I hoped that my planning and sweet gesture would pay off in my favor.

The next day came faster than I could have imagined. Maybe it was the nerves or going out on another date with Sundai. Maybe it was the fact that I knew she was heading home soon. This was my last chance to woo her, and I knew it. I knew her likes and dislikes. I knew her quirks and what made her tick. Her beauty was only the icing on a cake that I could indulge in forever. I laughed the first time Mrs. Opal mentioned setting me up with her daughter that I never met, but now I completely understood her point of view, and I didn't want anything else.

The grocery deliverer knocked on the door around eight in the morning. Kane let out a quick few barks, but I silenced him before going to the door. I prayed that he didn't jet out of the door and frighten the woman who was delivering my groceries. I couldn't imagine the fear and panic he would cause her.

"Just leave them on the porch. I don't want the dog to run out," I said to her.

She dropped the bags and retreated to her car in understanding. I was sure that she encountered this type of thing all the time, and she was grateful for the heads up. A few whimpers let me know that the big baby of a dog needed to handle his business. I ensured that the delivery driver was gone before I attached his leash and headed out of the door with him. A few laps around the block, and he was satisfied. We turned back onto the street and headed towards the house. To my surprise, Sundai was standing in the door. She waved eagerly as we approached.

"Good morning," the sound of her voice was chipper, and her smile was brighter than the sun that shone down on us.

"Hey," I said as I walked over to the porch.

I stopped at the bottom step, though. I had business to take care of, so I wasn't going to stick around to socialize. It was going to be hard, but I had to prep, nonetheless.

"How are you feeling this morning?" I asked her.

"I'm here. I didn't sleep very well, but I'm okay."

"I'm sorry to hear that. Do we need to postpone our date?"

"No," she said, "I don't think so. What time should I be ready?"

"I was thinking noon, but I didn't know what time your flight was."

"I can fly out at four, so noon works for me."

"See you soon," I said to her before turning to leave.

I walked across the grass and driveways that separated my house from Mrs. Opal's. I let the dog in before grabbing the bags and heading inside. I double checked to make sure everything was there that I ordered. I didn't have time for an error on behalf of the grocery store. I poured dry kibble into the plastic bowl that I had set aside for Kane, but he plopped down on the kitchen floor. I went to work slicing some fresh fruit. I started with a banana, some strawberries, an apple, and a peach. I placed them all into a clear Tupperware container and snapped the lid closed. I moved on to dicing up some cheddar and Colby jack cheeses. They went into another container with some red and green grapes. I rolled up some ham and turkey slices and speared them with toothpicks. I grabbed a variety of chips, crackers, and nuts next. I had enough food for what I had planned, but I wanted to include something sweet. I searched the bags for the remaining items. I didn't know what she liked, so I bought Oreos, Chips Ahoy cookies, and brownies. I packed everything into their designated containers, and carefully placed the containers inside of a cooler bag.

Noon rolled around quicker than I expected, but I was ready. I loaded everything up in the trunk of my car. I checked my reflection in the mirror that hung in the hallway of my house. The guy that looked back at me was confident. I wore a white, linen button up shirt with matching shorts and a pair of Sperry's. It was a casual but yet comfortable outfit. I felt like I looked good, and Sundai would appreciate it. I grabbed my white Panama hat with the navy-blue ribbon that circled the crown. I dabbed on some cologne and pranced out of the door. It was time.

As I approached her door, Sundai stepped out onto the porch. The smile she wore caused a smile to spread across my face. She was dressed in a one-shoulder sundress. The baby pink fabric cinched around her waist and flowed effortlessly to the floor of the porch. Her hair bounced in loose curls around her shoulders. Her make-up choices were light and accentuated her natural features. She looked amazing and smelled like a mixture of fruits and berries. I was impressed.

"Wow."

"Too much?" she asked sheepishly, "I can change."

"It's perfect. You're perfect. Ready to go?"

I extended my arm in her direction, and she took it enthusiastically.

The ride to our destination took over twenty minutes, but the sounds of K-Ci and JoJo crooned through the speakers of my car. The smooth R and B set the tone as I stole glances at Sundai. I noticed everything about her from how she bopped to the music to the French manicure and pedicure she wore. I pulled into one of my favorite places in the city and parked—Williamson Park.

"Our date is here?" Sundai asked as she glanced around the park. A feeling of anxiety mixed with fear set in as she spoke the words.

"Yes. I hope that's not a problem."

"It isn't. My mom used to bring me here all the time when I was younger."

"Mine too."

I could see the sadness resonate on her face at the mention of her mother. I understood how she felt. My mother passed years prior, but it was a wound that never healed. It was just something that you learned to live with. I knew all too well how she felt. Mother's days and my mother's birthday were two days that the band-aid fell off, and it felt like some dumped salt into the wound.

I often stayed to myself for that very reason. I knew the pain of losing a mother, and a part of me hated that Sundai was having to deal with it. She was such a beautiful woman, but the sadness often overcame her, and her mood changed in a matter of moments.

"You, okay?" I asked, but I knew that she wasn't.

She took a few deep breaths and forced a smile before saying, "Yes. Let's go."

I grabbed the cooler bag and a blanket from the trunk of my car, and we walked a short distance before we came up to the perfect spot. The grass was plush, and the spot was shaded by a huge oak tree. I spread the blanket out and began to unpack the goodies from the cooler bag. I took note of her expression as I laid things out for her. She was bottling up emotions and masking them with a smile. I didn't say anything about it at first, but I made a mental note to ask her about it later. She took a seat on the blanket, and I served the food that I packed up the previous day.

"So," I said trying to break the ice, "tell me about yourself."

CHAPTER 22

Sundai

I was surprised to my core that Bryce planned a picnic for me. He didn't have much time to get things together, but somehow, he managed to pull it off. I stood there and watched him spread a blanket on the ground and unpack containers that contained random types of food. I was excited because I hadn't eaten anything yet, so I was ready to smash whatever he brought. I stood patiently while he set everything up, and then took a seat on one side of the blanket, careful not to disturb anything. I crossed my legs and waited for him to hand me a small plate of assorted goodies. I didn't know how I felt about him fixing my plate, but I chalked it up and smiled as he handed it to me.

"So, tell me about yourself," he asked as we began to snack.

I removed a toothpick from a slice of ham and sandwiched it between some crackers. I took a bite of it before I answered his question.

"hmmmm," I started, "Well, I'm sure my momma told you a lot already."

"That's true," he said with a laugh.

He started to eat his own food, but I felt like his question deserved a little attention at least.

"I'm a broadcast journalist, but I also love reading books and doing puzzles."

"What's your favorite color?"

"Navy blue."

A laughter erupted from his throat that almost caused him to choke on whatever he was eating. It made me feel some type of way. I didn't understand what was so funny, so it made me feel like he was laughing at me instead of laughing with me. I cocked my head to the side as a slight attitude set in.

"I'm sorry," he spit out quickly, "I wasn't expecting that. Most women would say pink, purple, yellow, or something. Navy blue caught me off guard."

I shrugged my shoulders and let the attitude roll away before I spoke. The last thing I wanted was for it to come across like I was upset or mad when I really wasn't.

"Well, I guess I am not like other women."

"That much we can agree on."

"My birthday is next month. September 20th. I'm a Virgo, and our birthstones are sapphire. Navy blue is the closest to sapphire, so it's my favorite," I explained.

He nodded his head in understanding. I took a few more bites of my food and he followed suit. A moment of quietness circled us, but I refused to let it drown out the moment.

"So, what about you?" I asked.

"Well, I'm a high school teacher and football coach. Kids are my life. I don't have any of my own, but I treat all of them like I birthed them."

"That's admirable. Do you want kids one day?"

"I do, but I have to find the right woman to have them with. I am looking to wife a woman, not turn her into a baby mama with an army of my kids running around."

I already knew that Bryce was a good guy. He came in and uplifted me in what could easily be described as one of the toughest times in my life. He was a ray of sunshine in the darkest of times, so that spoke volumes about his personality. Hearing him describe wanting to make some lady an honest woman made me smile inside and out.

"What type of woman do you like?" I asked.

He paused for a moment in deep thought before he answered, "Someone who is honest and trustworthy. I want to give her my all, but I need to know that she's mine and not every Tom, Dick, and Harry that she comes across," he started, "also someone who is intelligent and has goals and dreams, someone who lets me be the man in the relationship, and if she can make biscuits like Mrs. Opal that would be a plus."

"Well, count me out," I told him, "I don't think I can perfect her recipe."

We shared a laugh as we both returned to our food. I popped a couple of club crackers in my mouth and struggled to swallow.

"I appreciate the array of food, but I don't see anything to drink here," I said to him.

"I didn't forget anything," he said.

He reached into the cooler bag and emerged with a chilled bottle of raspberry Sparkletini, and two plastic wine glasses emerged from the side of the bag. He poured one for me and one for himself. I took a sip from the glass and the bubbles tickled the tip of my nose. A smile spread across my face as I couldn't contain the happiness that I felt. It was a nice contrast to the overwhelming grief and sadness I had been feeling since my mother passed. It was nice to be able to breathe even if it was for one afternoon.

"I hope you find her. I really do," I said to him after the crisp wine washed down the food, and I was able to speak again.

He didn't respond, but I could tell by the glimmer of sadness in his eyes that he felt like that somebody would be me. In another time or a perfect world, maybe. I didn't see anything wrong with Bryce. He was ridiculously handsome and seemed to have his head on his shoulders right. My mother loved him, so that was almost enough for me. I refused to give up on my dreams, though.

The rest of the picnic was as nice as it started. We finished eating, had dessert, and packed everything away. We were on our way back to my mother's house when his true feelings emerged. I wasn't sure if it was the wine that had him feeling outspoken, or if he wanted to give it one last shot before I climbed out of his car.

"Sundai, I really like you," he started, "It's a shame that we can't work something out."

"I know. Come to New York, and I'm all yours," I said jokingly.

"Do you need help getting to the airport?"

"No, my car is already packed. I will make it. Thank you for such a beautiful picnic. Thank you for helping me get through all of this," I said.

"Anytime."

With that, I climbed out of his car and hopped right into my own. I would be a liar if I didn't say I was ready to be on my flight and headed back to life as I knew it. I waved solemnly at Bryce as I backed out of my mother's driveway. I glanced in the rearview mirror and realized that he was still standing there staring at the car drive away.

My mind was in shambles. I came home to bury my mother not to find a love connection. I knew the old adage that love would find you, but I wasn't that person. I didn't believe in fairy tales. Life was lifing, and I felt like I didn't have the room or energy to pursue anything with Bryce. I knew that it was a punishment of sorts. All he did was show up and try to comfort me. He tried to fill the obvious voids in my life, but I just kept meeting him with wall after wall after wall. It didn't exactly make me feel good about myself, so I wouldn't relax until I was onboard the plane heading back to life as I knew it.

CHAPTER 23

Lucas

I woke up the next day with a lot on my mind. It was my birthday, but I wasn't thrilled about it. I woke up from a crazy dream that left me sitting on the side of the bed in my hotel room. You know, the ones that seem so real that it makes every part of your body react. You wake up breathing hard, brow sweating, and disoriented. In my dream, I was in a physical battle with Kieli and Alaisha. They were ripping me apart piece by piece, and before the last dismemberment took place, I was startled awake. I sat on the edge of the bed with my head resting in my hands. I didn't know the exact meaning of the dream, but somehow, I felt like one or both of these women were going to be the death of me. I slid from the edge of the bed and slinked to the shower. In my mind, I would wash the bad vibes away from me and get on with my day.

I decided to skip breakfast, lunch or any other instance that might cause me to run into Alaisha. I even considered getting a room in another hotel. The suite I was in was comfortable, but that comfortability came with a major headache. The sex with Alaisha was magnificent, but it was apparent that she wanted more. I didn't know if I was prepared or able to give her the relationship that she wanted. The water from the shower cascaded down my body as I thought about her. Even when I didn't want to think about her, she occupied space in my mind. I couldn't help it. I knew what she wanted. Deep inside, I wanted it too. There wasn't a man alive that didn't want a good woman. We were designed to have queens—women that loved us, respected us, and sexed us whenever and however we wanted. I had no doubt in my mind that she could be that woman. The doubt had nothing to do with her and everything to do with me.

I climbed out of the shower, dried myself, and dressed in the outfit I had planned for the day. It was my day, but there weren't any spectacular plans. I was just going to kick it at Bryce's house, so there was no need to dress up. I slid into a pair of Levi's, a t-shirt that featured a blue and white Jordan 23 logo. I had a matching French blue pair of Jordan 13's sitting by the wall waiting to accentuate my outfit. I checked out my outfit. It wasn't too much, but I felt like I looked good.

I managed to get out of the hotel without running into Alaisha, and I said a prayer of thanks for that. It was after three in the afternoon, so I figured that she was off work and minding whatever business she had. I pulled my rental car into the familiarity of Bryce's neighborhood. The smoke that billowed from behind his house let me know that he already had the grill up and running, and I was appreciative. I climbed out of the car and knocked on his front door before I let myself in. I found Bryce in the kitchen shaping a few burgers for the grill.

"Heyyyyy," he sang out in greeting as I walked into the kitchen.

"What's up?" I said as I reached my fist out to dap him up. His hand was full of ground beef, so he extended his elbow which I touched to mine.

"Need any help?" I offered.

"Nah. The ribs, chicken, and sausage are already on the grill. I'm gonna throw these on there when there's room," he said as he motioned to the meat he was working with.

"Dang. Who are you cooking all this food for?" I asked and

waited patiently for his answer. I knew I mentioned that I didn't want a party but leave it to Bryce to throw me one anyway.

"Just us," he answered, "wasn't that the plan?"

I nodded my head and grabbed a cold beer from his fridge. I snatched an apple from a fruit basket that was situated on his kitchen island before following him out the backdoor. I was shocked to see a massive behemoth of a dog tied to a tree in his backyard. He raised his head when he saw me walk out onto the patio, but he didn't seem threatened by me at all. I took a seat as Bryce manned the grill. As soon as my ass hit the chair, he assaulted me with a plethora of questions.

"So, bro," he started, "When are you going to get your life together? Where's Shawty from Chill? Aren't you tired of being single?"

I inhaled deeply and took a deep swig of my beer. I didn't want to tell my brother to shut the hell up or tell him that he was ruining my birthday already. I didn't want to talk about any of his subject matter. I simply wanted to kick back, drink some beers, and eat some tasty food. I should have known that all of this was going to be too good to be true. He saw me out with one woman, and now we were rehashing the "Lucas you need love" conversation that weaseled its way up every now and again.

He took a sausage from the grill and wrapped it in a slice of white bread and passed it to me. I was grateful. The scent of food was awakening my hunger and reminding me that I hadn't eaten anything. The apple that I was nibbling on did nothing to stifle the hunger pains I was feeling. I tossed it into the yard, and it landed a few feet away from the day. I watched as he rose from where he was lying to investigate. After he sniffed it for a few moments, he turned saddened eyes to the patio, and his expression was read loud and clear. He would have preferred for me to have tossed my sausage and not the apple, but I had no intention of giving it to him. I took a few bites from the sausage and stared out into the yard. I was hoping that the pause and silence would encourage my brother to move on to something else, but I was wrong. The longer I took, the longer he waited.

"I don't know what you want me to say," I started, "you know what Keili did to me."

"We're still stuck on that bitch?"

It surprised me to hear Bryce talk like that. He was too proper and too chivalrous to call a woman out of her name. I guessed he felt the same way about Kieli as I did.

"Listen, she is out there living her best life. How long are you going to let this woman and what she did to you control you?" he asked.

"Control me?"

"Yes, every moment you drag this on you are giving her power over your life. I'm not saying that you need to forget, and I'm definitely not saying that you need to forgive her. I'm just saying that you're my brother, and you deserve to be happy too."

"I am happy."

"I'm not talking about this make-believe shit you are trying to put on. I mean really happy," he pushes.

"You mean like this make-believe shit you put on, brother?" I asked. The entire conversation put a sour taste in my mouth, and I tossed the rest of my sausage to the dog. He accepted it graciously and scarfed it down in a matter of seconds.

Bryce stilled, and I can tell that what I said struck a nerve. I didn't intend for it. He started it though. I just wanted to chill. He wanted to host an intervention of some sorts, so I was going to play his game.

"You sit in this house and bury yourself in your work. Day in and day out. Then a woman comes along and spreads your bell pepper nose wide open, and you let her leave," I say to him.

The mention of Sundai caused his breathing to hitch. I saw the emotions in his eyes, and I felt bad. The sparkle in his eyes was inevitable. I didn't know how to feel about it. I didn't see him act like this about any other females. He didn't bring any females home for holidays, and he never spoke about going on dates. He didn't brag about them because there weren't any dates to brag about. I was really starting to worry about him, so to see him in his feelings about Sundai was a breath of fresh air.

"I didn't chase her because she has her own life to live," he said, but I felt like there was more to it than that.

"Plus," he continued, "I didn't know what to make of you two."

"Us two?" I asked with an obvious look of confusion on my face.

"Yea. The whole airport thing. I didn't know who to believe."

"Nothing happened between Sundai and me," I reassured him, "I was just salty when I saw her sitting there with you at that restaurant. I'm sorry."

My apology was lackluster, but I hoped that it hit where it was supposed to. Through it all, he was my brother. I never intended to drive a wedge between him and Sundai—especially if there were genuine feelings involved. Based upon the goofy expression on his face, there were definitely some feelings involved. The dog stirred from his position and let out an exasperated howl. It was as if he was cosigning in our conversation, and I laughed. We both laughed, and the moment was lighter and airier than the one before it. I was glad.

An hour and a few beers later, I was tipsy and sitting on Bryce's couch as he fixed a plate of food for me. He suggested I eat something to soak up the beer that flowed freely in my system. He placed a plate in my lap. There were ribs, chicken, baked beans, pasta salad, and a little green salad as well. I knew that my brother could cook, but I didn't expect him to go all out for just the two of us.

CHAPTER 24

Sundai

T hings were finally getting back to normal. Well, as
normal as possible. I drowned myself in my work, and it
helped me not to think about the grief and pain that
was associated with losing my mother. Everyone offered their
condolences at the time. They were all sorry for my loss and had
all types of well wishes and prayers. No one told me that the grief
never went away. It didn't get easier at all. There wasn't some
magic remedy for the days when I cried myself to sleep or for the
days I wanted to pick up the phone and call Opal and couldn't.
There was no cure-all for those days, and those were the days that
I buried myself deeper in my work. It was a suitable distraction.

I woke up and got myself ready for work. It was the beginning of football season, so I knew that the station would be
buzzing with people. There were coaches and players to inter-
view, and the sports section had new reporters and anchors that
couldn't wait for their few minutes in the spotlight. I dressed in
an olive-green pants suit complete with an ivory shirt beneath it.
I gelled my hair up into a high bun and put on a pair of gold
hoops and a gold necklace. It was one of my favorites. My

mother gave it to me one year for my birthday. It was a gold butterfly that was enclosed in clear rhinestones. The butterfly dangled from one of its wings, and I always joked that it looked like it was going to fly away at any moment. I slathered my favorite lip gloss across my lips and felt like I looked good. I was satisfied with my look, so I headed out of the door and drove straight to work.

I walked into the station and into a reception that I was not expecting. It was as if people were standing around waiting for me to walk in. They all erupted into a chorus of "Hey Sundai" and "I'm so sorry for your loss." I knew I had all of their condolences. They sent flowers to the funeral home that expressed it, so I knew. I didn't want to be rude though, so I took a moment and hugged and interacted with them all. It didn't do much for my mental health as I was trying to push my mother's death to the back of my mind. I didn't want to forget it. I simply wanted a distraction.

I eased my way through the crowd and walked into my designated filming area. I took a seat behind the circular desk. Behind me, the green screen that normally showed the station logo was down and ready for the day. I sat in my ergonomic chair and waited patiently for the day to begin. The station assistant came running into the studio with a cup of coffee in hand.

"I'm sorry," she began, "I didn't know you were in here. I would have had your coffee waiting for you."

"It's not a problem. Thank you, Samantha."

I took a sip of the warm liquid, and it instantly warmed my body. Maxwell House original roast with two spoons of sugar and a healthy serving of Crème Brulee flavored creamer. It was the same recipe that she had been brewing up for me since I started my job. Most people ordered some sophisticated drink from Starbucks or Dunkin Donuts. I wasn't that bourgeois, nor was I that much trouble. She kept a coffee pot in the studio just for me, and I appreciated it. I heard footsteps approaching, and I knew that they belonged to the camera man, production manager, and anyone else that was needed to get this show on the road. I inhaled deeply and asked myself if I was ready to be back live again. I shook off any doubts as the studio lights brightened, and my co-host, Tyler Moody took his seat on the stage.

"That's all the news I have for today," I said thirty minutes later, "Now, let's turn our attention to the skies and find out what mother nature has in store for us. Over to you, Paige, with the latest on the weather front."

After reporting on local campaign efforts, a string of car break-ins, and an inspiring story of an elderly woman who was rescued from her burning home, I was happy to turn the broadcast over to the meteorologist. I sat in place with a smile transfixed on my face until I saw the red lights of the camera flash off indicating that we were no longer live. The production manager, Angela, confirmed that we were off the air before I released the breath that I hadn't realized that I was holding.

"Great first day back, Sundai," she complimented me before exiting the studio.

"Well, if it isn't the illustrious Sundai Johnson," a deep baritone said from somewhere in the studio.

The studio lights were still on, and I couldn't see much beyond where they stood. As if they were a part of my thought processes, the lights clicked off. It took my eyes a moment to adjust, but once they did, I was able to see the person who walked into the studio and addressed me. I was speechless for a moment as the gentleman stood there and stared directly in my direction. He stood well over six feet tall and was dressed in a tailored suit. He exuded confidence and strength as his eyes bore into mine. He was well groomed, and his appearance spoke volumes about the type of man that he was. I was slightly confused though. He knew who I was, and I didn't know anything about him.

"Nice job today," he said to me as he approached the desk where I was still sitting.

"Thank you," I said with a confused expression that was mixed with a pleasant smile.

Truth be told, I didn't know how to feel. The handsome stranger strangled me with the scent of his cologne, but I liked it. His presence alone made me smile, but he reminded me of Bryce.

That part alone made me want to get up from the table and run away. As much as I wanted to run, I wanted to sit there and pick his brain. He came into my studio for a reason, and my nosey ass wanted to know what that reason was. There were several other studios in the building, and he could have gone in any of them, but instead he was standing in front of me.

"I'm sorry. I know this was rude of me. I'm Quincy Anderson," he said as he extended a hand in my direction.

I took his hand and shook it. He held it a little longer than necessary while I tried to figure out why his name was ringing bells in my head. I felt like I should know who he was, but the trauma I had been through with my mother was clouding any other information.

"I'm sorry?"

"Sorry, I'm one of the new sports broadcasters," he responded.

"Right, I remember seeing an e-mail about you being hired before I went home to bury my mother," I admitted.

"Yes, about that," he said, "I am so sorry for your loss."

I groaned internally. I was so tired of hearing that it wasn't funny. I found myself faking politeness and biting my tongue. No one knew what I was going through or how I felt, and I struggled to hold it in the road.

"Thank you," I said quietly, "It's nice to meet you. How's the job treating you?"

"It's been great, but it's better now that I have gotten to meet you. I watched you on television before I applied here. I was hoping to meet you. This is the highlight of my day," he said as a smile spread across his face.

I gushed a little with a smile of my own, "That's sweet."

"I was hoping I could take you out to lunch," he suggested.

I hesitated for a moment. I didn't know what his angle was. I was still grieving, and a part of my mind was still reeling over Bryce. No matter what I chose to think or how I chose to act, I left a part of my heart in Cooperville, Alabama. I stared at Quincy and saw a glimmer of hope in his eyes, and it scared me. I wasn't trying to jump into a relationship, and I definitely didn't want to build a relationship with someone I worked with. I had never done that before, but I knew that it never ended well. Things could get extremely messy, and I didn't have the time or patience to deal with the messiness that almost always ensued.

"I don't think so," I finally answered, "thank you for offering though."

"Come on," he insisted, "No strings attached. Just a friendly lunch between two new coworkers and new friends."

He flashed a smile in my direction, and I couldn't help but notice how straight and white his teeth were. Everything about him attracted me, and that worried me to my core. I saw red flag after red flag, but I became Ray Charles and turned a blind eye to everything that worried me.

"Fine," I conceded, "What did you have in mind?"

"Whatever you have a taste for."

"I really have a taste for soul food," I said thinking that I would name something that he couldn't provide. I had been in New York for years, and I was yet to find a place that cooked good soul food.

"I know a place," he said," It's not too far from here. We can walk over after your noon broadcast if you want."

I nodded my head in agreement, but I couldn't help but give him a weird side eye. He seemed to have had everything planned out, and that was the part that I didn't like. I was very untrusting, and I wondered if I had a good reason.

The noon broadcast came and left just as quickly. It was a recap of the stories I shared during the morning broadcast. The only difference was the segment that reported a few traffic accidents that had occurred since the first broadcast. As always, I completed my broadcast and waited patiently to be counted down. The same countdown that indicated that we were offline any other time. The same countdown that I heard every other day, but this day it lagged and seemed to go by in slow motion.

Once everything was wrapped up, I grabbed my pantsuit jacket and hung it over my shoulders. I walked to the door of the studio, and a part of me hoped that Quincy changed his mind or ghost me. I would be perfectly fine with that. I would hop down to the sandwich spot down the block, grab a quick bite, and be A-okay. All of my plan b thoughts went out of the window when I smelled his cologne as soon as I walked out of the studio door. He was standing against the wall with one leg propped up. He looked comfortable like he had been waiting in that position for a moment. He smiled as soon as he saw me, and it made me feel some type of way. Butterflies were unleashed, but I tried hard to tame them as I approached where he was standing.

"Ready?" he asked.

I nodded my head, and we took off walking through the station and out of the front door. The weather was clear, and it was a wonderful day. I didn't mind the walk, but I prayed that it wasn't far. I wore cute shoes that were not made for walking. We went a few blocks before he stopped in front of a three-story building. The first floor was a Mexican restaurant that I was familiar with.

"I didn't know Fiestas sold soul food," I said to him.

"They don't," he replied, "Be patient."

He led me to a narrow staircase that was located near the entrance of Fiestas. He opened the door for me, and I waited for him to take the lead inside of the lobby. I had no idea where we were going and what he was up to, so I stood patiently until the door closed and he walked ahead of me. He took the stairs two at a time, but I refused to. The pumps I was wearing wouldn't allow it anyway. My mind was reeling, and the last thing I needed was a misstep and for me to go tumbling down the stairs. We made it to the first landing, and he opened that door for me as well. As he did, the smell of fried chicken and other things wafted in the air. It appeared that we were on a floor that housed apartments, and I was even more confused than before.

"I know you didn't just trick me into coming to your house," I said as my feet froze in place.

"No, not my place," he answered, "trust me."

I didn't know his ass, so his use of the words "trust me" had no bearings on how I felt. I couldn't believe I fell for this shit. I knew that I was familiar with the area, and I knew there wasn't a soul food spot in the vicinity. I fell for his chiseled frame and bright smile, and now I was standing there half irritated.

"You wanted soul food. Let me deliver," he said.

My mind was telling me to turn around but the more I wanted to, the more the scent of food was drawing me in. I was a fatty, and I was never prepared to turn down good soul food. We passed a few doors, and finally he came to a stop in front of a door, and the smell of food was outrageous. My stomach growled ferociously as he knocked. I held my breath and waited to see who opened the door.

My heart leapt into my throat when an elderly woman wearing a moo-moo answered the door. Her hair was tied up in a matching head wrap, but her bangs hung from the bottom. She smiled from ear to ear when she saw us standing there.

"Hey, Q Baby," she said as she pulled him into a tight hug.

"Hey, nana," he said as he rested in her arms.

Nana? I thought to myself. *Is this his grandmother?*

"Nana, this is my co-worker I was telling you about, Sundai," he said as he broke out of her embrace, "Sundai, this is my grandmother, Earnestine."

"Hello, ma'am," I said to her as I extended my hand in her direction.

She grabbed my hand and pulled me into a hug similar to the one she had just given Quincy. It caused me to laugh out loud. She reminded me of Opal, and it warmed my heart.

"We don't shake hands around here," she said, "you're about to eat my food, so you are family."

"Yes ma'am."

She walked us into her dining room, and I couldn't help but look around her home as I walked through. Her home was sparkling clean. There didn't seem to be a speck of dust or anything out of place. Quincy and I sat across the table from each other while Ms. Earnestine fixed us heaping plates of food.

"I didn't know what you liked, so I made a variety of stuff. If you don't eat anything, just let me know," she said with a warm smile.

"I eat everything except fish," I told her.

"Great."

She moved around the house with skilled precision and placed plates in front of me and her grandson. There were collard greens, rice and gravy, oxtails, macaroni and cheese, a chicken leg, and a cornbread muffin. I didn't know where to start. I bowed my head as Quincy blessed the food, and then we dug into the meal that his grandmother had prepared.

"Mmmm. This is so good," I said as I shoveled macaroni and cheese in my mouth.

"I told you I knew the best spot," Quincy bragged.

"Yea, but I never would have guessed that the perfect spot was your grandmother's house," I admitted.

"Honey, I watch you on TV," she admitted," you're always welcome in my home."

"Thank you," I said courteously as I continued to eat.

When we were done eating, Ms. Earnestine emerged from the kitchen with a Pyrex dish that smelled like peach cobbler. I couldn't see inside of it, but the notes of cinnamon and peaches hit my nose simultaneously.

"I hope you saved room for dessert, dear," she said to me as she spooned cobbler onto some saucers for us.

"I didn't, but I can't turn down peach cobbler. I haven't had homemade cobbler since my mother made it," I said.

The mention of my mother opened up a floodgate of emotions. I sat at Quincy's grandmother's dining room table and fought an emotional battle that neither of them knew about. I spooned the warm cobbler into my mouth and as soon as the flavors burst onto my tongue, tears burst from my face. I let out a gut-wrenching sob that drew Ms. Earnestine and Quincy's attention right to me. I had a mouthful of peach cobbler, and I was crying my eyeballs out. I swallowed the dessert before swiping at my face.

"I'm so sorry," I tried to apologize for my random outburst of emotions.

Ms. Earnestine dropped what she was holding and made her way around to my side of the table. She wrapped a comforting arm around me. It wasn't as awkward as I expected it to be. Instead, it was comforting. I melted into her arms and the scent of Red Door swarmed around me.

"It's okay, child," she said, "I know how you feel. These are tears of pain. Your heart is broken, and you need to get it all out."

I opened my mouth to say something, but she kept talking. The vibrato of her voice was soothing as she held me like I was her child. She held me how I would imagine she would hold Quincy if it were him that was crying.

"I was young when my mother died. I don't remember it, but I lost my child. Quincy's mother died young, and it was a pain that I can not describe. I lost myself in the grief for a while, but I eventually had to emerge from it so that I could take care of Q," she said.

I glanced through teary eyes across the table, and Quincy offered an understanding smile. I felt embarrassed and broke the hold his grandmother had me in. I was invited over for lunch, and here I was sitting here bawling like a little baby. I couldn't believe it myself.

"I can't believe this," I said out loud, "I was invited over for lunch, and here I am drowning in my own tears."

"Child, this is a no judgment zone. You've been holding on to this for too long. I can tell. You've been trying to be strong, and the entire time you needed to be weak. You needed to cry, and it is okay."

I wiped the remainder of the tears from my face as she packed up the leftover food into two to-go plates. She handed one to me and one to Quincy. I was so appreciative of her maternal influence. It was my first time meeting the little lady, but I felt like I needed to meet her. Opal used to say that everything happened for a reason, and I didn't doubt that there was a reason for me meeting Quincy's grandmother.

CHAPTER 25

Bryce

How do you manage to get someone off your mind that you genuinely cared about and liked? I secretly wished there was a handbook to the shit. I'd fly down to the Cooperville City library, check it out, and read it backwards and forwards. No such book existed, though. Without it, I was stuck in a weird headspace. I was lost between trying to forget her and wanting to pack up my entire life to go find her. Every free second of my day revolved around her, and regardless of what I tried, I couldn't get her out of my mind. In the brief time that she was here, she had made that much of an impression on me. It was pitiful. She was gone, and so was Lucas. All I had to distract me was work and Kane.

It was late on a Friday afternoon—well after the last bell rang at Cooperville High. I stayed behind to fill out some paperwork and straighten my office. Both were things I had neglected during the day. When I finally climbed into my Toyota Tundra and headed towards home, my feet hurt, and I was exhausted. As I turned into my street, a car parked in Ms. Opal's driveway caused my heart to flutter. I hurried up and jumped out of the car with a renewed sense of energy. I barely put my truck in park before my feet hit the pavement. I took a few deep breaths and calmed myself before walking towards her house. As I made it to the door, it swung open. I expected to see Sundai, but instead a chocolate woman who was about my height stepped out on the porch. My presence startled her, and she lost the grip on the clipboard she was holding. Papers scattered across the porch, and I struggled to grab them before the wind caught them and carried them away.

"I'm so sorry. I didn't mean to scare you," I said sincerely.

"It's fine," she said as she adjusted the skirt she was wearing and took her papers from my hand, "thank you."

"You're welcome. I was hoping the homeowner was here. I live next door," I explained.

"Ah, I see. I'm sorry to disappoint you, but Sundai is not here. She was adamant about not coming back until it was absolutely necessary. She asked me to handle everything."

"Handle everything?"

"Yes. I'm Grace Anderson with Grace Realty. This house is currently on the market," she explained.

"Damn, she's selling it?"

I heard what she said, but I didn't want to believe it. I know she mentioned it, but I didn't think she would actually go through with it. I figured she was grieving and speaking out of emotions. I thought she would want to hold on to something of her mother's. I guess I was wrong.

"She is. I'll be over here assessing the house for a while, and I'll be in and out for a few weeks until it's sold," she announced to me, and I felt like that was my cue to leave her to her business.

"Understood."

I nodded my head in her direction and easily withdrew myself from her business. I headed towards my house, but my mind was elsewhere. I couldn't believe that Sundai was really selling the house, and I couldn't help but think that Ms. Opal was disappointed. Hell, I was disappointed.

Once I was inside of the comfortable atmosphere of my own home, I filled Kane's food and water bowl. I thought he'd want to go outside but he didn't budge when I grabbed his leash. He lounged lackadaisically on the dog bed that he was really too big for. It was big enough to hold his torso, but his rear legs hung off the back of it, and his head and front paws rested on the floor in front of it. I made a mental note to buy him a bigger one as soon as I was paid again. I was glad that he opted not to go out right at that moment. I didn't want to run the risk of running into Grace again, and it gave me a moment to rest my feet. I grabbed my tablet before reclining in my chair.

I googled Sundai Johnson and was instantly surprised when her photo popped up. It was a professional photo, but her smile was bright and seemed to radiate from her eyes. She seemed happy, which made me happy. There was a newspaper article attached, and I didn't hesitate to open it and read it:

In a glittering ceremony last night, broadcast journalist Sundai Johnson took center stage as the recipient of the prestigious "Visionary Voice Award for Distinctive Broadcast Impact." This accolade recognizes Johnson's exceptional contributions to the realm of broadcast journalism, applauding a career marked by unique storytelling and influential reporting.

The Visionary Voice Award, presented annually to individuals who redefine the landscape of broadcast journalism, serves as a testament to Johnson's commitment to delivering news with depth and impact. Colleagues and viewers alike lauded the journalist for her ability to transcend the ordinary, offering audiences a fresh perspective on pressing issues.

In her acceptance speech, Sundai Johnson expressed gratitude for the honor, emphasizing the power of journalism to effect positive change. "Every story is an opportunity to connect, to bridge under-standing, and to inspire change," she remarked.

As Sundai Johnson adds the Visionary Voice Award to her list of accolades, the broadcast community eagerly anticipates the continued brilliance and distinctive impact she will undoubtedly bring to the world of journalism.

I was taken aback and wowed by the article and couldn't believe that Sundai was making such a splash. My heart swelled and my chest burned with pride as I stared at the photo. I only had the pleasure of knowing her for a short while, but I was proud of her, nonetheless. I saved the article and forwarded it to my work email address. I would print it when I was back inside of my office.

I wanna do something to congratulate her. I thought to myself. I wasn't sure what, though. I thought long and hard about a gesture that wouldn't come across as creepy or stalkerish. A few minutes passed by before I decided to send a bouquet of flowers to the news station where she worked. Ms. Opal has mentioned it as being WXNY in New York. I looked them up, and luckily their address was listed on Google. I smiled to myself and was happy as I saw bits and pieces of a plan unfolding in front of my face.

CHAPTER 26

Sundai

Monday morning, I walked into work as I would any other day. My confidence was through the roof. Maybe it was the navy-blue body con dress I wore and its white geometrical pattern. The dress was paired with a navy-blue suit jacket and a pair of blue flats. My hair was pressed to the Gods and hung just below my shoulders. The white accessories I wore set everything off. There was a white Marc Jacobs bag on my shoulder and white pearls on my wrist, neck, and ears. I looked like a million bucks. If it wasn't for the outfit, maybe I was still skating on a high from winning the Visionary Voice Award. It was normally given to broadcast journalists with mountains of experience and years under their belt. I didn't have a ton of either, but apparently, I was making waves in the industry. Forget making a splash, everyone was starting to know who Sundai Johnson was, and I loved it. Samantha approached me with a cup of coffee as soon as I made it to our work area. She was beaming with a smile that was almost as bright as mine.

"Good morning and congratulations."

"Thank you, honey!" I said to her.

"I have a bouquet of flowers that came in for you today. They're gorgeous too!"

"They are probably from Quincy," I speculated, "just put them on my desk."

She nodded her head and turned on her heels. I rolled my eyes, but quickly adjusted my mood. Nothing and I meant nothing was going to ruin my day. I felt like the flowers were from Quincy because he had been trying to lay it on thick since we left his grandmother's house. He was doing entirely too much which caused me to pull away and distance myself from him. Ms. Earnestine's food was some of the best I had ever eaten. He was right about that, but it wasn't enough for him to woo me out of my drawers. I knew that's what he wanted, so I fed him out of a long-handled spoon. I saw him whenever I wanted to. I made it my business to avoid him. He went left and I went right. I didn't want to be mean or rude to him, but I secretly wished that he would get the hint. I hoped that he would crawl into whatever hole he emerged from. My two broadcasts went by without incident. Nothing was spectacular about my day. Tyler had an attitude that threw me off a little, but I managed to ignore him. I knew that he was a little irritated that I was chosen for the Visionary Voice Award and not him. He didn't try to hide his disdain, but it didn't bother me in the least bit. I noticed it, but there was nothing he could do to ruin my mood or bring me down.

After the noon broadcast, I walked out of the studio in an attempt to make a beeline for my office. I was moving so fast that I almost ran into Quincy. He was dressed in a black suit with silver pinstripes. His black and silver tie coordinated with his suit perfectly. I groaned to myself but tried hard to steady my face. I attempted to hide how I was feeling, and I prayed that my face wasn't revealing the emotions that were swirling inside of me. He had a pan of something in his hands, and it smelled like his grandmother's peach cobbler. He had my full attention.

"Congratulations," he said, "my grandmother made this pan of cobbler for you."

"Thank you, Quincy but this is too much."

"What do you mean?"

"You already sent me a bouquet of flowers. Now you're bringing me Ms. Earnestine's cobbler," I said to him.

"The cobbler is from Nana, but I didn't send you flowers," he responded.

"You didn't?"

"No."

"Please thank your grandmother for the cobbler for me."

He nodded his head, and I took the mini aluminum pan out of his hands. I turned and made a beeline for my office. I didn't stick around to talk or hear anything else he had to say. Once inside of the safety of my office. I closed the door and slid down into the chair behind my desk. It took a few minutes for me to calm down and catch my breath, but once I did, I surveyed the items that were on my desk. Everything was normal except for the most beautiful bouquet of flowers I had ever seen in my life. The glass vase held navy blue roses and sunflowers. The combination was different but beautiful, nonetheless. There was a navy blue and yellow ribbon tied around the vase that matched the flowers inside of it. I scanned the flowers for a card and any indication of who may have thought enough of me to send the flowers. I noticed it sticking out of one side of the bouquet. I snatched it out quickly and read it. The message was short, simple, and straight to the point:

Congratulations. I am so proud of you. Bryce.

His name—five letters that caused my heart to palpitate. Every emotion I tried to force behind my wall of security began to break through. Brick by brick it was slowly but surely being broken down. I just knew that he moved on with his life. I just knew that he didn't think about me anymore. I also knew that the news of the Visionary Voice Award was not announced in Cooperville, Alabama, which meant that he had to look it up. I crossed his mind, and he looked for me. I felt my cheeks flush with emotion, and I struggled not to cry again. Every day and every situation seemed like a battle not to cry. I had never been too sensitive, but the death of my mother seemed to bring that side out of me. I sniffed the sunflower closest to me and committed the scent to memory. They smelled wonderful, and I was surprised that he thought enough of me to send me flowers. I thought my abrupt leaving would turn him off and make him forget about me. I thought he would erase any trace of me from his memory, but the flowers were an obvious sign that he didn't.

I leaned my head against the back of my chair and closed my eyes. As I did, I saw his smile behind my eyelids. I thought about the picnic he planned for me before I left Alabama. My eyes snapped open, and I glanced at the flowers. The flowers and the ribbon were navy blue. I vividly remembered him laughing when I told him that my favorite color was navy blue, but he remembered. He remembered, and ordered flowers that he knew I would love. They meant so much more to me after I realized that he chose the shade of blue on purpose.

As I stared at the flowers, a knock echoed through my office. I wondered who was at my door. Anyone who needed me normally called or e-mailed before disturbing me in my office.

"Come in," I said.

The door swung inward, and I found myself face to face with Quincy. He walked into my space and sat at one of the white leather chairs that were positioned on the opposite side of my desk. I froze momentarily as I tried to figure out how "come in" translated to "sit down and make yourself comfortable."

"What's up?" I asked.

"Did you enjoy the cobbler?" He asked.

"I haven't eaten any yet. I was going to stop and get a pint of vanilla ice cream and enjoy it when I get home," I informed him, "Please make sure you tell your grandmother thank you for me."

"You can tell her yourself when you come to dinner on Sunday," he suggests.

"I can't," I said quickly, "I don't even think that's a good idea."

"What is it about me that repulses you?" he asked, "Is it because I didn't send those flowers? Or is there another man in the picture?"

"Neither one, actually. I'm just not that interested."

"I had you all in my grandmother's house. Do you know how many people I take to my Nana's house?" he asked as the hurt flashed across his face.

"Prayerfully none, but keep in mind I didn't ask for that. That was your idea, and I am grateful for the opportunity to meet your sweet nana. I really am, but you will not hold that over my head."

He shook his head as if he couldn't believe the words that were coming out of my mouth. He rose without another word and walked out of my office just as he had come. I didn't care. In fact, I was relieved. I was over him, but I still planned to enjoy my pan of peach cobbler later.

Good riddens. I thought to myself.

Even though I didn't care for Quincy, I thought his grandmother was the sweetest person I had met in New York City. I made it my business to stop by her apartment when I got off of work. I felt like Quincy was going to be thwarted and forget to tell her what I said about the cobbler, and I was raised better than that. I passed Fiesta's just like I did the day I went to her apartment with Quincy. I climbed the stairs anxiously and knocked on the door.

"Who is it?" her little voice called from the other side of the door.

"Sundai Johnson, Ma'am," I said politely.

Before I could get the words out good, the door swung open and Ms. Earnestine stood there with a huge smile plastered on her face.

"Are you here for Quincy?" she asked, "I can grab him."

"Uh, no ma'am," I said hurriedly before she had the opportunity to call his name, "I just wanted to stop by and tell you myself how appreciative I am for the cobbler."

"You're welcome baby. I saw you won that big award on t.v., and I knew I had to do something for you," she said.

I smiled at the sentiment, and it caused her to smile as well.

I turned to leave, and I heard his voice from the back of the apartment.

"Who's at the door, grandma?" he called as he strolled into view.

His eyes met mine, and a glimmer of hope shimmered in his. He hadn't expected me to show up at his grandmother's house again, and that was obvious.

"Thank you again, Mrs. Earnestine," I said to her, "Have a good evening."

I turned and flew down the hall, leaving her and Quincy to whatever discussions they were bound to have about me.

CHAPTER 27

Lucas

The trip to Alabama for my birthday was refreshing. I was happy to see my brother. We used to be so close, but time and distance pulled us apart. I had a fit to move to New York to chase my dreams, and my brother refused to stop me. I possessed our father's ear for music, and our mother's voice. Singing and playing the acoustic guitar were two of my passions, and I didn't feel like I was being heard in Alabama. I chose to move to New York City, and my brother encouraged me every step of the way. I didn't tell him that I hadn't had a gig in months, though and I was running low on cash. I almost didn't fly home for my birthday, but it had become an annual thing for us, and I refused to ruin it.

I glanced around my one-bedroom studio apartment. It was nothing like the home my brother lived in, and a part of me felt foolish for moving halfway across the country. I knew that people did it all the time, but I hadn't heard the horror stories of people who went broke and ended up homeless in Central Park. I felt like I was a month or two away from being homeless, and Bryce had no idea. I didn't know if I even wanted to tell him. I knew that he had a vision when it came to his brother, and I didn't want to be the one to ruin it for him.

I rolled out of bed and flicked the light switch. I thanked the good Lord above when I flicked the switch, and the lights came on. I knew that the bill was due, and I had no idea when they were going to disconnect the power. I knew that there wasn't any food in my refrigerator or cabinets, so I grabbed a cup of ice water and lounged on the couch. I didn't know what else to do, so I broke down and dialed Bryce's number. It was early, so I figured I would catch him before his classes began.

"Yo, bro," he said, answering the phone, "what's up?"

I skipped the pleasantries and went exactly into what I called for.

"Listen, I need a huge favor. Can you loan me eleven hundred dollars?" I asked him.

"Eleven hundred dollars?" he repeated, "for what?"

I broke down and explained my situation to him. There was a deafening silence on the other end of the phone, and I couldn't tell if he was listening intently or trying to formulate a quick solution. I hoped that he wasn't silently judging me for all of the decisions I made in my lifetime. He was always the more successful brother. He seemed to have it all together, and everything fell right in line for him from the moment he graduated high school. I always felt like if our parents were here, Bryce would be their pride and joy. I would be the black sheep and the son that caused them to shake their heads whenever they thought about me. I would be the one to put a sour taste in their mouths. I never intended for it to be that way, but at the same time I wasn't a good fit for the mold they had in place for their children. I was content blazing my own trails and chasing my dreams.

"Bryce, are you there?" I asked hesitantly.

"Yea."

He let out a deep sigh before he spoke again. I could hear the disappointment laced in his tone as he did.

"Why didn't you tell me what was going on when you came on your birthday? Why even come? You could've used that money elsewhere," he said to me.

"I could have. You're right, but I needed an escape, and I needed to be around my brother. Is that a crime?"

"Nah, I guess not. I just don't want you up there struggling," he said, and I could hear the sincerity that now flowed freely in his voice.

"So, can you loan me the money?"

"I can, but that is a temporary fix. What are you going to do next month and the month after that?"

Honestly, I hadn't thought that far ahead. I hoped that something would work itself out for me, but if it didn't, I didn't know what the next step was going to be.

"I have an idea," my brother said after another brief silence.

I didn't answer him right away. Instead, I gave him the opportunity to keep speaking so that he could divulge whatever idea it was that popped into his brain.

"You know Sundai's mother passed away when she came home. Her house is for sale. It's right next to me, but it'll be a house, nonetheless. We can buy it, and you can move home," he said, "that is if you don't mind living next to your brother."

I didn't even think about his suggestion for a second. It made me laugh out loud even though it wasn't a comical situation. I knew that he was serious, but it didn't make sense to me.

"Bro, I'm telling you that I can't afford to pay my rent, and you expect me to pay a mortgage every month?" I asked skeptically.

"Maybe. Maybe not," he replied, "I may be able to work something out for you."

"Something like what?"

"Let me check on some things, and I'll call you back this evening after work."

We disconnected the call, and I breathed a healthy sigh of relief. I wasn't sure what Bryce had up his sleeve, but I felt like he would help me work it out.

CHAPTER 28

Bryce

A fter the call with Lucas, my chest tightened. I couldn't believe my ears. I knew that he was going to New York to pursue a music career, and I remembered telling him that it was a stretch. I expressed my feelings and tried to persuade him to stay in Alabama, but his spirit was too wild and free. He wanted to go, so I stood by and watched him leave.

I finished getting ready for work, and made sure Kane was good before I walked out of the door. Before I pulled out of my driveway, I noticed the for-sale sign at the end of Ms. Opal's driveway. Along with the sign was a plastic caddy that held flyers. I jogged across the lawn and grabbed one out. I read it and took notice of all of the specs of the house. Grace highlighted the major attractions of the house, and I hoped it wouldn't draw too much attention before I could put my ducks in a row. The price for the house was listed at $130,000, which I felt was extremely cheap for a house in our neighborhood, but I didn't complain about it. I knew that Sundai was simply trying to get the house off her hands, and I would gladly take it.

The day went by fast. The students were nonchalant, and I made it my business to leave as soon as the last bell rang. There was no detention or anything that held my attention after hours, so when the last bell rang, I locked my office door and walked out with my students. I accessed my bank account during my lunch break, and I was ready to call Lucas back and let him know the plan I had for him. I didn't know if he would go for it, but it was worth the shot, nonetheless.

I pulled my Toyota Tundra into the driveway and noticed that Grace was back at Ms. Opal's house again. She climbed out of her car as I climbed out of mine. She waved gingerly in my direction, and I walked across the grass to intercept her steps.

"Good Afternoon, neighbor," she said as I got closer to where she stood.

"Hello," I said, "Please call me Bryce."

"Okay then, Bryce."

"Have you had any bites on the house?" I asked and stood eagerly waiting for her response. I wondered if she would respond, or if she would try to gaslight me into thinking that there were a lot of potential buyers.

"Not the first," she said.

"Really?"

She shook her head intently, and in that moment Ms. Opal's smile crossed my mind. The wind whipped around us out of nowhere, and it made me feel like she was giving me the push that I needed to go ahead and speak up when it came to her house.

"I'd love to buy it," I said to her.

"Have your bank contact me with your loan information," she said as she checked the flyer caddy to see if she needed to add more flyers to it.

"There won't be a loan or a mortgage," I informed her, "I can get a check, money order, or cashier's check. Whichever you prefer."

She stopped what she was doing and turned to face me. Her mannerisms completely changed right in front of my eyes. She went from being preoccupied to showing me her full and undivided attention.

"I'm not sure I heard you correctly, Sir."

"Bryce."

"I'm not sure that I heard you correctly, Bryce," she repeated, "Are you saying you have $130,000 on hand, and want to purchase this house?"

"Precisely," I said to her, "$150,000 if we can close in two weeks," I said to her as I stared directly into her eyes.

We stood there and hashed out a few more details before she handed me her card which I accepted with a promise to call her in the next day or so to finalize things and start the process.

I tied Kane up in the backyard and slouched down in one of my patio chairs. Sitting out there reminded me of when I was out there for Lucas' birthday. I hadn't been out there since, and it was nice to sit out and enjoy some fresh air. I pulled my phone out of my pocket and dialed my brother. He answered after two or three rings.

"Hey, Bryce," he said into the phone, "What's up?"

"I told you that I would call you back when I got off work this evening. I have a solution to your problem."

"Lay it on me, but it better not be that house next door to you. I told you that I cannot afford it," he said.

"You don't have to. I have some money saved up. I can front the bill for the house. I even talked to the realtor, and she's willing to work up a deal, so we can close in two weeks."

My brother let out a cough that sounded like he was struggling to breathe. I wasn't sure if he was okay or not. I didn't even know if it was something that he would agree to. I just took it upon myself to get things going like I knew he was going to agree to move home.

"Hello?" I interjected into the silence.

"So, you're just going to buy me a house?" he asked, "it seems a little good to be true."

"Nah, it'll be my house, but I can't stay in both of them."

"What's the catch?"

"I'll help you with utilities until you find a job, but you will need to find a job," I said, "Oh, and take that nice woman on a date. A real date."

I threw the last part in there jokingly. I knew he'd never agree to it, but I threw it in for shits and giggles. His response shocked me to my core, though.

"Deal."

CHAPTER 29
Sundai

I was two steps outside of the studio from our morning broadcast when my cellphone rang. I snatched it out of my purse and couldn't contain the excitement when I saw Grace's name and number flash across the caller ID. I hired her to handle the sale of my mother's house because she was one of the top real estate agents in the area, and I knew that she would get it handled for me.

"Grace," I said, answering the call, "please tell me that you have some news for me."

"Actually, I do. I have a potential buyer for the house. He's offering twenty thousand over the listing price, but he has two contingencies," she explained.

"Contingencies? What does that mean?"

"The buyer has two things they are requiring for the sale to go through."

I trudged through the news station as my attitude emerged from the depths of me. I didn't know what the buyer could possibly be trying to demand, but it already irked my soul. I just wanted to be done with the entire situation. The more I held on to my mother's house, the more I was reminded that she wasn't living in it. Her oven wasn't baking biscuits, and her garden wasn't thriving in the backyard. It was painful, and I wanted to be done with the entire process.

"What are the contingencies?" I asked as I burst into my office door.

The flowers from Bryce were still holding on to life. Every time I saw them, I smiled as bright as the sunflowers that were positioned throughout the bouquet.

"The buyer wants to close in two weeks, and they ask that you are present at the closing meeting. They don't want to close via fax or anything else."

"And they are paying $150,000?"

"Yes ma'am."

"Fine. Let me know the date and time, and I will be there. I have some more time I can take off of work, but I am glad that this will be over and done," I said to her.

"I completely understand," she said, but I didn't actually think she did.

"I'll shoot you over an e-mail when we hang up with all of the details."

I agreed, and we disconnected the call. I checked my e-mail a few minutes later, and I could feel the color drain from my face. I scanned her e-mail and paused when I got the purchaser's name. There in black and white was a name that caused me to freeze. The e-mail quoted the buyer as being Bryce Nathanial Alexander. *It can't be.* I thought to myself. I didn't know his full name, but I didn't want to believe that my mother's neighbor and the man that tried so hard to get my attention was the same man that was buying my mother's house. I tried to shake the thoughts out of my mind, but it was virtually impossible. Bryce was on my mind more than a little bit, and there wasn't much I could do to get him off. He was implanted there, and I didn't know how to feel about it.

Two weeks went by, and I found myself back on a plane heading back to Alabama. I never imagined that I would be going back so soon, but I chalked up my feelings and did it anyway. I felt a weird mixture of feelings, and I didn't know how to handle them. There was an anxiety when it came to possibly seeing Bryce again, and that scared me. Before I could figure it out, it was smothered by the grief and mourning that was associated with my mother. Even her name caused pain. I heard her voice all the time and saw her face whenever I closed my eyes. For the first few days after her passing, I would smell her perfume at the most random of times. I found myself crying more and more. I was a fragment of my old self—the old self that was happy and carefree all the time. I used to smile and really meant it when I did. Now, anytime I smiled it was a frail attempt to cover up the feelings that were coursing around inside of me. I didn't have anyone to help me through this, so I put up a wall and plastered a fake smile onto my face. They always say, 'fake it until you make it,' and I wondered if I faked my happiness long enough if it would make me genuinely happy one day.

The airport had a rental car company situated right inside its doors. It was the same rental company I used last time, and the same one I would use this time as well. It was convenient. I could pick up my car and go, and when I came back, I could easily drop the car off and leave. I checked in and waited patiently while the attendant went to retrieve the car that was reserved for me. Sooner than later, a black Kia Telluride zoomed to a stop in front of the building. I requested an SUV, but I wasn't expecting a Telluride. It was my dream car, so I knew that I was going to enjoy driving it around Cooperville even if it was only for a few days. I headed straight to my hotel room to freshen up before I walked into Grace's office. I needed a breather and an outfit change before I handled business.

The meeting was scheduled for four pm. I walked into her office exactly two minutes after the hour. Grace was sitting behind her desk tapping lightly at the keys on her keyboard. Two chairs were positioned opposite where she sat. One was empty, and the other was occupied by my mother's old neighbor, Bryce. I sucked in a deep breath when I saw him. I knew that it was a possibility, but I didn't think that this Bryce and that Bryce were one and the same.

"Sundai, so glad you made it in safely," Grace said, breaking into the thoughts that were marching across my mind, "how was your flight?"

"The flight was fine," I said to her.

"Hello, Sundai," Bryce spoke calmly, but I could tell that he was stifling his excitement.

"Bryce," I said to him as I took a seat in the chair next to him, "So you're buying my mother's house?"

"I am."

"Why? Don't you have a house?"

"It's for my brother, and plus I don't think Ms. Opal would want her house being sold to the highest bidder," he said, but instantly looked like he regretted saying it.

He sat there looking like if he could have sucked the words back up, he would have. It was a simple statement, but it hit me like a bag of bricks being tossed around by a tornado. The wind felt like it was knocked out of my body. I couldn't believe that he had more care about my mother and her belongings than I did. Here I was trying to sell the house and move on, and his thought processes were the exact opposite. I shook my head in disbelief, and for a moment, I had cold feet about selling the house.

"Are we ready to get started?" Grace asked as if she could feel the hesitation that I was sure was radiating from me.

I took a millisecond to think about what I was about to do. It was permanent, and there was no going back from it. I considered both sides of the coins when it came to selling my mother's house. It was one of the only things I had of hers besides a few pictures and some memories, and the only thing I could think of was getting rid of it. For a brief moment, I felt ashamed of myself and like my mother was ashamed of me too. I held on to those feelings for a second too long and forced myself to swallow hard. I fought the tears that were threatening to fall and glanced around the room. Grace and Bryce had both focused their attention on me. I knew that they were waiting on me to say something. The meeting would not start until I said something. I needed someone else to take the lead on this one, though. My mind seemed to be in a million places at once, and my heart seemed to be ripping in half. I knew that I didn't have the time or energy to maintain the house. The best thing would be for me to sell it.

"We don't have to do this if you don't want to," Bryce said. The calmness in his baritone worked as an anchor to pull me back to the present. I felt like my breathing was returning back to normal, and the tears were receding. It was something about his voice and his presence in general that calmed me.

"No, we can proceed," I spoke finally, "I am sorry."

Grace nodded her head and began to read the crucial details of the agreement out loud. I nodded my head in agreement every once in a while, to urge her to continue. The sooner I could sign the paperwork and collect my check the better. The sooner I could get out of there. When she was done, Bryce and I went to work signing papers. I received a copy of the papers and Bryce received one as well. He handed over a cashier's check that he was holding when I walked in. I didn't notice it until he went to pass it to Grace. She in turn passed him the keys to my mothers house. The house where I grew up, and the house where Opal died.

"Is there anything else?" I asked, "I need to get out of here."

"That's it. I'll take my fee out of this payment and forward the rest to you," she said, "give me two to three business days."

"I will be in town for two days. It would be nice if I could get it before I leave," I told her.

"I will see to it," Grace responded.

Bryce extended his hand in my direction. I didn't really want to shake it, but I figured it was the professional thing to do. He took my hand in his and gently shook it. I couldn't deny or ignore the spark I felt when my skin made contact with his.

"Can I take you out to lunch to celebrate?" he asked me.

"There's nothing for me to celebrate," I said as I snatched my hand out of his and walked out of Grace's office.

CHAPTER 30
Lucas

P acking and moving home was easier than I expected. I had a few pieces of furniture, but the bulk of my items were clothes and shoes. Bryce had everything shipped to my new address, and a week later, I was stepping foot into my new residence. I wasn't sure how to feel about it. A part of me felt like a failure. I never wanted to give up and return to Cooperville. In my eyes, I was going to be the next world renown music star, and I couldn't wait to tour the world and play on international stages. I guess that it was time to hang that dream up and focus my sights on something more practical—something that made sense, and definitely something that paid the bills.

"Welcome home," Bryce said as I stood in the middle of the living room.

I responded with a smile. I wasn't sure what else to say. The entire move was overwhelming, and it happened so fast. I knew that it was for the best, but it was going to take some getting used to.

"What are you going to do now that you are home?" he asked.

"I am going to start by putting in some job applications," I responded, "you have done so much, and I think it's time for me to stand on my own two feet."

"Sounds like a solid plan, but I'm here to help if you need me."

"Bryce, you're a high school teacher and coach. I know you are not rich," I said with a little more attitude than I meant to. I wasn't trying to be an asshole, but I didn't want him blowing smoke up my tail pipe either.

"I'm not rich, but I have a substantial savings and as long as I'm working, I add more to it."

I nodded my head in understanding, but I still made up my mind that I was going to find a job as soon as possible. I wanted to stand on my own two feet. I was a man, and I wanted to be the man of my own house.

The next day came, and I heard Bryce's old truck crank and leave. I knew that he was headed to work, so I took it as a sign that I needed to get up and make something shake. He had given me a few dollars before he left the house the day before, and I wanted to make sure I put them to good use. The first stop was McDonald's. I was craving a sausage and cheese McGriddle. There were plenty of McDonald's in New York, but I rarely got to step foot into one. I handled my morning hygiene, dressed, and hopped right into my Nissan Altima. It was the same car I had since my junior year in college, but she was still running. "Lucy" as I called her had gotten me to more than a few point A's and B's.

I drove right to the closest McDonald's and ordered my breakfast via the drive thru. I sat in the parking lot and scarfed the sweet breakfast sandwich down. I chased it with an orange juice before moving along to my next stop. The hotel across the street from McDonald's was the same one I stayed at during my birthday week—the same one that Alaisha worked at. I wasn't going to approach her right away, but the more I sat across the street staring at the building, the more courage I built up. I crunk Lucy and jetted across the street, and before I knew it the cool air of the lobby was greeting me. The doors of the Oasis slid open, and I saw her as soon as I stepped into the foyer.

"Welcome to the Oasis," she said without looking up from the computer in front of her.

She was dressed in a beautiful dress that featured black, gold, and white swirls of color. A black and gold cardigan covered the dress. She was dressed modestly, but it was something about her that stuck out like a sore thumb. Her hair was pulled up in a low bun that rested against the nape of her neck. She even wore a pair of gold hoops and a gold necklace. I stood there and stared at her. I felt something in the pit of my stomach, and I couldn't recognize the feeling. I guess it was what people in the books and movies described as butterflies. I never felt this feeling or anything like it with Kieli. I tried to turn around and walk out of the same door I came in, but I moved a few minutes too late.

"Lucas?"

I heard her voice say. It was something about the tone that turned me around instantly. Her eyes met mine, and her expression willed my feet to move forward. I cleared the space between the door and receptionist desk in what felt like a few seconds.

"What are you doing here?"

"Can we talk?"

"What is there to talk about? You said all you had to say the last time you were here," she snapped out.

She was right, and I deserved every single ounce of attitude that she was prepared to dish out. I had been nothing but cold to her, and she didn't deserve it. All she wanted was someone to care about her, and that someone she wanted was me.

"You're right. I was a total asshole, and I apologize for that. It's a lot you don't know, and it's a lot I would like to tell you," I explained to her, "Can we talk?"

"I go on my first break in an hour," she said, "we can talk then if you want."

I nodded my head and began to map things out in my head. An hour left me enough time to go to the Cooperville Public Library to put in a few applications. It wasn't that far from where we were, so I would make it there and back in time to catch her break. It also gave me enough time to get my nerves and thoughts together.

"I'll be back," I said to her.

I drove the short distance to the library, and I was surprised that the parking lot was almost empty. The last time I was within the brick walls, they only had about ten computers. I wasn't sure if they had upgraded in the years I was away, but I was excited to know that I wouldn't have to wait long for a computer. As I stepped foot into the library, I was overcome with the familiar smell of old books. The scent was a nice combination of earthiness and muskiness. The old wooden floors creaked as I walked through the library. It was the only sound that broke through the quiet environment. Shelves and shelves of books towered over me as I headed towards the neon green sign that read "Computer Lab." I was curious and wanted to stop and check out some of the books. In my younger days, I was an avid reader of thrillers and fantasy, but I hadn't had a physical book in my possession in years. Now that I was back home, there were a few books I wouldn't mind diving head-first into. The first was thriller by Nadia Nicole called Targeted.

I pushed the thoughts to the back of my mind as I walked into the designated computer area. An elderly gentleman sat at one of the computers and slowly pecked at the keyboard in front of him. He nodded his head in my direction as I took a seat at my computer. I sat there and searched the web for job availabilities in the Cooperville area. I filled out a few random positions here and there while keeping my eyes zeroed in on the clock. I was slightly distracted, but I wanted to get this done. Forty-five minutes and about fifteen applications later, I found myself headed back towards the Oasis.

When I walked in the door, Alaisha was assisting a guest at the front desk. I picked a table in the food service area and had a seat. The lady who was setting up for lunch completely stopped what she was doing and spun around to face me. A spark of recognition flashed across her face before she opened her mouth to speak to me.

"Hello, can I help you with something?" she asked with a smirk.

"No, thank you," I said to her, "I am waiting for Alaisha."

Her smirk evolved into a full out smile. She smiled like she knew who I was and why I was there, and my statement only validated her hunch. She turned back to her food just as I heard heels clicking against the tile of the floor. I looked up to see Alaisha approaching the table. She wasn't smiling, nor did she seem happy. I wondered if her mood was due to the day she was having or if she was feeling some type of way because I was there. I wasn't sure, but either way it made me feel slightly uncomfortable.

"You made it back," she said to me.

"I did. Did you think I wasn't coming?"

She let out a light humph, but she didn't confirm or deny it. I stared at her for a brief moment, and her gaze caught mine.

"Would you like to step into my office?" she asked as she gazed around the lobby and at her nosey coworker. I nodded my head and rose from the table.

We walked into her office, and she took a seat behind the safety of her desk. I leaned against the closed door and took a few deep breaths before either of us spoke.

"Lucas, I don't understand why you're here. You told me everything I needed to hear, and you made it crystal clear how you feel about me. You don't care." she said with an exasperated sigh.

"You're wrong," I began, "I do care. I actually care about you more than I have cared about anyone in a long time, but I can't shake this fear in my heart. My ex cheated on me, Alaisha. She cheated and it broke me."

I could feel my chest ripping open as I spoke to her. I felt exposed and like my heart was bleeding out and onto the maroon and gold carpet. I never had the notion to open up to anyone about how Kieli made me feel. In doing so, it made me come across as cold and distant.

"I get that Lucas, but what did I do to you? Is it fair to me or anyone else that you hold one person's mistake against us?"

I wasn't sure if she wanted me to answer her question or not, so I just stood against the door with my lips tightly pressed together. I felt lightheaded and like the air was slowly being sucked out of the room. I sunk down into one of the chairs across from her. I glanced up from my hands that were interlocked in my lap to the woman that sat across from me. She didn't want anything except someone to care about and love her. I wasn't sure why she had chosen me to be her person, but here we were. I searched her eyes for understanding, and I was surprised at what I found. The hard exterior of a pissed off woman melted away, and in its place was a vulnerable woman. I matched her level of vulnerability. The truth was we needed each other.

"You have no idea how much I want to be with you. I really do, but I'm scared of this," I said as I motioned between us, "I'm scared of opening up and being vulnerable, but I don't want to lose you because I'm letting the past control me."

"Then don't Lucas. I see something special in you. We can take it slow and build something real," she said.

My head hung and I broke the eye contact she was struggling to hold. I was grappling with my own insecurities, and it was easier for me to stare in my lap. My hands didn't judge me, and they definitely didn't pressure me.

"I want to try, Alaisha," I said to her, "But I need you to be patient with me. I'm still learning to trust again."

"I can be patient, Lucas. I care enough to wait. We can figure this out together."

I glanced up again and was shocked by what I saw. Her strength radiated through. She was willing to try, so I made up in my mind that I would at least meet her halfway and try too. In that moment, I realized that love was a risk that was worth taking. I couldn't let Kieli take the happiness from my life. I deserved to be happy, and I deserved to be loved. The room instantly became lighter as Alaisha smiled at me. It was a sweet, endearing smile. I smiled back and watched as she drew her bottom lip between her teeth and bit lightly.

"Don't do that," I warned her, "That shit is so sexy. I didn't come here for this, but you are going to make me bend you over your desk and show you how bad I missed you."

She smirked at me before she spoke, "I dare you."

CHAPTER 31
Alaisha

I knew better than to dare him. I knew exactly what was coming next, but I would be lying to myself if I said I didn't want to pounce on him as soon as he walked through the doors of the Oasis. The sexual tension was always there between Lucas and me. He always knew how to soothe it too, and I needed that. Spending nights alone with my rose vibrator was great, but that vibrator didn't throb with life, and it didn't tickle the spots that Lucas could.

As soon as the words escaped my lips, he rose from his chair, and I rose from mine. He was up on me, and I could feel his rock-hard body pressing against my soft one. He wrapped his arms around me and pulled me into a kiss. His lips met mine, and he took his tongue and parted my lips. I allowed them to part and allowed his tongue to rendezvous with mine. His strong grip held my body in place. He didn't want me to run, but little did he know I didn't want to run. I wanted this. I wanted him. The Lucas that stood in front of me was different. The animalistic man who was trying to get his rocks off and ghost me was gone. I could feel it. This version of Lucas, even though equally animalistic, needed me. He wanted me.

As if to show me how much he wanted me, his arms tightened

around my body as he kissed me again. My hardened nipples poked him though my dress. In one smooth move, he spun me around and lifted my dress until it rested around my lower back. My exposed ass was in the air, and I didn't care at all. I was grateful that I had chosen not to wear any underwear under my dress. It made for easier access. I didn't know that he was coming, but everything happened for a reason. He cuffed one of his biceps around my left leg and entered me in one quick movement. I wasn't sure when he managed to undress or if he even managed to slip a condom on. At that point, it was too late to be concerned with anything.

He slid in and out of my center while I reached for something to hold on to. I gripped the edge of my desk as he went deeper and deeper. His pace quickened, and my eyes rolled to the back of my head. Sex with Lucas was always amazing, but this session felt different. It felt like we were connecting on a level higher than physical. He was claiming me as his, and we both knew it. Echoes of my wetness and our skin slapping echoed around the office.

"mmm luc—" I managed to say before he slapped my exposed ass causing my words to get caught in my throat.

My hips met him stroke for stroke, and it felt like he was deeper than I ever imagined he could be. It felt like a dance of some sorts as he spun us around. He managed to sit on my desk with me on top of him without slipping out of me. I was amazed, but I didn't have a second to catch my breath before he was pumping into me from beneath me. It was my time to shine and took the opportunity to show him how bad I wanted this moment with him. I bounced in his lap and gyrated my hips to my own rhythm.

"Take this dick," he coached, "Show me who's dick this is."

The sound of his voice caused me to lose control. Every inhibition I had went out of the window as I gave him all of me. My brain short circuited as I twerked on his manhood. I gave him everything I had. I was putting on a show, and from the grunts and growls that came from Lucas I could tell that he was enjoying every bit of it. I wasn't sure how long we went like that before he was tapping my ass in submission. I climbed off of him in time to see his seed erupting from the mushroom tip of his penis. I struggled to catch my breath as he struggled to catch his.

"Damn, Alaisha," he said after a moment.

"That was amazing. Much better than the last time when you took my ass and had your way with it," I said to him.

He tucked his still semi-erect manhood back into his pants and fixed his clothes. It seemed like my words had put a damper on the mood. I didn't mean for that to happen, but it was the truth.

"I'm sorry about that," he said quietly, "It'll never happen again. I promise you that."

"I hear you."

"I'm serious. Want to grab dinner tonight? Better yet, want to come to dinner at my place?"

"Your place?"

"Yea, I have a house. My brother has been cooking for me. I'd love to repay the favor for him, and I'd love for you to be there as well," I said to him.

He seemed sincere, and I couldn't help but agree. Food was my love language.

"I can pick you up when you get off, and we can go to the grocery store together," he suggested.

"That's fine. I can leave my car here," I told him, "I get off at five."

The rest of the day went by fast. No one stirred in the hotel except Kendra, and her constant side eyes made me laugh. She acted as if she knew what went on in my office earlier that day. She probably did. She was nosey. I was in there getting my back blown out, and it wouldn't have surprised me if she were in the hallway with her ear pressed to my door. I made sure that Lucas and I were both dressed and put back together before we walked out of my office. He gave me a light peck on the cheek before he left, and I knew that Kendra's ass was somewhere peeking around a corner. I didn't see her, but I felt her energy.

The end of the day came, and I walked out of the Oasis. Lucas was parked in the drop off area, and he leaned casually against the passenger side of his car. He was dressed in a pair of jeans and a button- up shirt—a different outfit than the one he wore earlier, but it looked good on him.

"Hey," he said as I reached where he was standing.

He reached out and hugged me before opening my door and ensuring that I was safely inside of his car.

"How long have you been here?" I asked as he opened his door and got in.

"Not too long. How was your day?"

A sweet smile spread across my face. I couldn't believe I was with him, and I couldn't believe that he was really asking me about my day. I thought about how I wanted to answer his question. I wanted to say *it was awesome. I got some really great dick today*. But I settled for a quick, easy response.

"It was great," I said.

He took that response and took off towards the store. I glanced out of the window and watched the scenery as it passed. When we pulled up at the store, I expected to sit in the car as he went in and grabbed what he needed. He glanced in my direction when I didn't remove my seatbelt, and I noticed the obvious frown on his face.

"Come on," he said, "You don't wanna walk with me?"

I slid the seatbelt off and eased out of the car without answering him. It was obvious that he wanted me in his presence, so I would oblige without hesitation. We walked through the parking lot arm-in-arm, and he seemed happier. I was too.

"Anything you don't eat?" He asked as he perused the meat section, and I shook my head.

"I was thinking about frying some steaks and shrimp and making some loaded baked potatoes and a salad. How does that sound?" He asked him.

"Sounds delicious. Anything I can grab for you?" I asked.

"You can run over to produce and grab three potatoes if you want," he said, "the large baking ones."

I nodded my head and took off on my mission. The store

wasn't that busy, so I made it to the produce section in a matter of minutes. I searched for a few minutes before I found the potatoes that I was looking for. I grabbed a plastic baggie and picked three of the best potatoes they had. I grabbed a container of watermelon too. I knew that it wasn't part of the menu, but I hadn't eaten anything since breakfast. I was going to need something before the steaks got done. If Lucas didn't buy it for me, I'd buy it myself. I took my things and headed back to where I left him.

I found Lucas standing at the Butcher's counter, I assumed he was waiting for some fresh shrimp. My blood froze in my veins when I saw a brunette standing in his face. She was talking and slapping him on the shoulder like they were old friends. She seemed happy to see him, but it was obvious that the feeling was not mutual. The look on his face was a mixture of repulsion, and irritation. I knew right away who the woman was, and I wondered how this was going to play out. I had just gotten him to a place where he considered opening up to me. I silently prayed that seeing Keili wouldn't cause him to shut back down on me. I stepped closer to where they stood, and I could hear the conversation.

"I've been missing you," she said, "I looked all over for you, but I couldn't find you."

"I didn't want to be found, Kieli," Lucas said, confirming my suspicions, "Why were you looking for me? Where is Milo?"

"Milo left me."

Lucas left out a throaty laugh, and his eyes met mine. I didn't want to step into this conversation, but I winked my eye at him to let him know that it was okay. I was not mad—not at him anyway.

"So, let me get this straight. Milo left you, and you came crawling back to me. You must be out of your rabbit ass mind to think I'd come back to you. Do you know what your betrayal did to me? Do you?"

"No," she said quietly.

"It broke me past the point of repair. I thought I was irreparable anyway, but I've had a change of heart," he explained.

"Great, so we can work this out then?' Kieli asked with an expression on her face that let me know just how serious she was.

I told myself that I wouldn't butt into their conversation. This was before me, so technically it had nothing to do with me. I was tired of her, though. Just the short time I stood there listening had me ready to mop the store floor with her. The old Alaisha probably would have. That Alaisha that was raised in the streets and by the streets, but I tried so hard to suppress her. I tried not to get ratchet, but bitches like Kieli would surely bring the ratchet side of me to the forefront.

"Baby, I got the potatoes," I said as I positioned myself between him and her. I placed the bag and the watermelon into the cart before I turned to face her.

"Can we help you find something?" I asked her as I tilted my head to one side. I made up my mind instantly that her response would determine how I reacted to her. If she played it cool, I would too.

"I was just talking to my friend, Lucas," she said.

"First off, Lucas is not your friend. He stopped being your friend when you crushed his heart. The heart I am working so hard to put back together. So, neither one of us requires your presence. Please move around before I move you around," I said to her.

My eyes cinched and my shoulders squared. I was ready for whatever, but I had a feeling that it wouldn't come to that. She wasn't about the life I was, and she didn't want any smoke. She held up both hands in submission, and mumbled "have a nice life" before she tucked her tail and took off through the store.

"I am sorry," I instantly said to Bryce.

"Sorry? That shit was sexy as hell," he said with a laugh.

The butcher handed him a package of shrimp, and we were on our way too.

"I just didn't want you to think that I was a roughneck. I'm not out here popping off every chance I get," I said to him.

"She would have deserved it," he said, and we both laughed.

CHAPTER 32

Bryce

An immense feeling of pride overcame me when I stood on Ms. Opal's porch. I knew that the house now belonged to my brother and me, but I couldn't help but refer to it as hers. I knocked on the door and waited a few minutes for someone to answer. I could hear the constant chatter of voices from inside of the house. It was obvious that Lucas had company, and I thought about turning around and heading back to my own house. I knew he mentioned that he wanted to cook dinner for me for once, but I didn't know it was going to be a crowd. I was a homebody, and a little bit of an introvert. I didn't have to be around a crowd at all. I took a deep breath and tried to relax my nerves.

When the door finally swung open, Lucas was standing there with a huge smile on his face. I knew that he wasn't that happy to see me, so I was curious to see who else was in the house. He slid to the side and let me into the house, and the aroma of food was overpowering.

"Hello, Bryce," a light voice said to me, and I looked up to see the same woman from Chill sitting at the kitchen table.

Lucas combined some of his furniture with some of the furniture that was left in Ms. Opal's house. I knew that Sundai

134

didn't mind. She was going to gut the house and trash everything that was left in it. I told her to leave it. Lucas went through and kept what he wanted and threw the rest out. It was nice to see that he kept her kitchen table. It was the same table that I sat at and ate with her on many different occasions. It held sentimental values, so I was glad to see that it was still there.

"It's nice to see you again," the woman said, pulling me out of my thoughts.

"You, too," I said to her, "What's your name again, sweetheart? I'm sorry."

"No worries. I'm Alaisha. I don't think we were ever formally introduced."

"I don't think so either, but it's nice to meet you."

She paused from eating a chunk of watermelon to shake my hand. I looked over at my brother who went to check on the food he had on the stove. His look said it all. He was happy, and that's all that mattered to me.

"So, guess who we ran into today at the grocery store," Lucas said as he flipped over a steak in the pan.

I took a seat at the table next to Alaisha, and she offered me a piece of her watermelon. I took it graciously. Watermelon was one of my favorite fruits, but I knew that she didn't know that. She rolled her eyes when Lucas mentioned the person from the store.

"Who?" I asked even though I felt like I didn't want to know.

"Kieli's trifling ass, and she had the nerve to try to get back with me. Milo left her high and dry, and she wanted to come home like she didn't cheat on me with my best friend."

"Boy, I wish I was there," I said, "I would have told her a thing or two."

"No need. Alaisha told her what she needed her to know. She's such a firecracker," he said, and he stood there smiling like a proud boyfriend or husband.

I wondered what the extent of their relationship was, but I knew that when it was time for him to tell me he would. I was simply happy to see him enjoying her company. I hadn't seen him smile as much in an extraordinarily long time, and the feeling caused a warm and fuzzy feeling to radiate through me.

"Speaking of firecracker," Alaisha spoke, "When's the last time you saw Sundai?"

My brother plated the food and set dinner in front of us. He took his seat, and we blessed the food before digging into the meal he had prepared. A few cuts of steak and a spoonful of my potato, and I hoped that the food was ample distraction from the question she posed. I felt like if I chewed long enough, then we would bypass that question and move on to something else. Lucas took that as his opportunity to answer the question.

"He hasn't seen her since he bought this house," he explained, "he let her get away again."

"What else what I supposed to do?" I asked, "she has her own life to live, and it isn't here in Cooperville."

"That's bullshit," he said blatantly, and he was right. He knew it and everyone else at the table knew it as well.

"Well, what do you suppose I do then, Lucas?"

"Go after what you want man. Isn't that what you told me to do?"

His words struck a nerve. The pot was calling the kettle black not long ago. I was telling him that he needed to approach Alaisha, and here I was not taking my own advice.

"Pretend I'm Sundai," Alaisha said, "What would you say to her?"

I turned in my chair to face her but hesitated before I said anything. She nodded her head, encouraging me to continue. I took a deep breath, formulated my thoughts and words, and spoke.

"Sundai, every time I close my eyes, I see your smile. All of my dreams revolve around you, and then my heart is broken repeatedly because you're not here. I love everything about you, and I need you in my life. I don't care if you're in Alabama or if I'm in New York. It doesn't matter as long as we are together."

There was so much more I could say, but I stopped and glanced around the table. My brother's expression was shocked, and Alaisha looked like she would burst into tears at any moment.

"That's so sweet," Alaisha finally said, "she needs to hear this. What's the problem?"

I shrugged my shoulders nonchalantly. I really wanted to change the subject. I didn't agree to come to dinner to be put on the spot like I was.

"How's the job hunting going, bro?" I asked.

"I did a few job applications today. Maybe someone will call me soon," he answered, "I was hoping I could find something music related."

A literal light bulb went off in Alaisha's head, and I could see the idea formulating in her eyes. I wondered what was on her mind, but I wouldn't have to wait long to find out.

"Music related?" she asked.

"Yea, I sing and play the acoustic guitar," Lucas said to her.

"My job just opened a bar with a pretty large stage," she told him, "we were looking for a permanent gig to play nights and weekends. The pay would be fairly good, but at least it would be something to keep the money flowing until you find something else."

"I'll take it," he said.

The rest of the meal went off without a hitch. The company and the mood were a beautiful vibe, but I had a lot on my mind. Their words resonated with me and made my heart swell. I wanted Sundai, so I knew what I had to do.

Fall break rolled around and gave me the perfect opportunity to travel. I had never been to New York, but I had the perfect reason to go. I purchased a plane ticket and took Kane to my brother's. He seemed happy to be in his old home, but my brother didn't seem thrilled about the arrangement. He felt like he owed me, so he didn't complain to me, but I knew the truth.

The day of my trip came, and I was shaking in my boots. I walked through the airport to the appropriate gate. Before I knew it, I was on the plane and needed something to calm my nerves. I flagged the nearest flight attendant down and asked for a strong drink.

"Here you go, sir," she said as she placed a cup in my hand.

I took it down in one gulp and prepared myself for the trip ahead. I focused on the end result, and the thought of Sundai in my arms lulled me to sleep.

CHAPTER 33

Sundai

Two weeks and $150,000 later, my mother's house was off the market. Bryce bought the house, and I still hadn't decided how I wanted to wrap my mind around that. I remembered walking into Grace's office and seeing him sitting there. He was as handsome as the first day I met him. A lump formed in my throat when I saw him, but I forced myself to swallow it down. We were there to sell my mother's house—nothing more and nothing less. So much so that I quickly declined his invite to go out. I didn't want to but the wall that was protecting my feelings was back in place, and I intended for it to stay that way. I waited around to collect my check, and then it was back to New York. I didn't hesitate to leave. As far as I was concerned there was nothing left in Alabama for me.

A lone tear rolled down out of the corner of my eye, and I quickly swiped it away. I was sitting in my office between live broadcasts, and the last thing I wanted was to go on live television with red and puffy eyes from crying. I sucked it up just as the phone started to ring,

"This is Sundai," I said as I answered the phone.

"Ms. Johnson, there is a visitor for you at the front desk," Samantha's voice sounded over the phone.

"I'll be right there."

I checked my face in a compact mirror that I kept in my desk drawer. It didn't look like I had been crying, and I appreciated that. I applied a little lip gloss to my lips and walked out of my office. I took the elevator down to the first floor. The ride seemed quicker than normal, but the door dinged and slid open alerting me that I had arrived. I stepped into the lobby, and there weren't that many people in the lobby. I wondered who was there for me, but my question was answered a moment later when I stood face-to-face with him. He was dressed in a navy-blue suit which instantly put a smile on my face.

"Bryce, what are you doing here?" I asked as I walked closer to where he stood. My heart thumped loudly in my ears as I got closer to him.

He smiled from ear to ear as I approached. I noticed a sparkle in his eye. It was the same look he gave me the day of our picnic in the park. He had waited for this moment, and all of his waiting was paying off.

"Sundai, I am here because I can't stop thinking about you. You told me to come to New York if I wanted you, and I realized that I do. I want you, Sundai."

My knees weakened, and my heart was filled with conflict. I took a few deep breaths in an attempt to steady myself, but it didn't work. The pair of dark brown eyes that I stared in seemed to swallow me and all of the emotions that I felt. I stood trans-fixed, and I couldn't break the trance if I wanted to.

"Bryce, you can't just fly across the country for someone you barely know."

"I know it seems crazy, but ever since you left Alabama, my life hasn't been the same. You're in my thoughts every day, and I can't let this chance keep slipping away from me. I need to know if there's a chance for anything between us."

The sincerity in his voice took me by surprise. The vulnera-bility in his eyes rattled something inside of me, and I could feel the wall breaking down again. It was something about this man, but he had that effect on me whenever I was in his presence. I could feel the tears starting to form again. I shook my head in a frail attempt to shake them away.

"I left Alabama because it was too emotional for me to stay. I can't believe you flew across the country for me, though."

"I know it's a lot, and I understand if you're hesitant. I can't pretend that I don't feel something for you, and I wish you'd stop pretending as well. I want to give this a chance, Sundai, so I was willing to take that risk," he said to me.

"You're crazy. You know that?" I said with a slight giggle.

"Maybe I am. But sometimes, you have to be a little crazy to find something extraordinary. I would have been a bigger fool if I didn't come," he explained.

That was it. The last brick that was separating Sundai Johnson from my heart and my feelings disintegrated. The levee that was holding my tears burst open, and they flowed freely down my face. My heart felt like it was beating a million beats per minute. Everything was happening so fast, but in that moment, I could hear Opal's voice. I called her one Sunday afternoon, and the only topic of conversation was Bryce.

"My neighbor is such a good man," she had said, "I told him he would be perfect for my daughter."

I scolded her for dibbling and dabbling in my love life, but she laughed it off and told me that someone had to. She said I would be the little old lady who lived in a house with a million cats if it was left up to me.

"Let love find you, Sundai. It'll be the most unexpected moment when it does. It'll feel like a gentle breeze that weaves its way into your life. Enjoy the magic it brings and the joy you feel," she had said.

That woman was wise beyond her years, and everything she said was happening. The breeze was named Bryce, and he blew all the way in from Alabama to put a smile on my face. The smile that was slowly spreading across my face mimicked the joy that was spreading through my heart and soul.

"Alright, Bryce," I finally spoke, "Let's see where this takes us."

Epilogue

"**G**ood Morning, New York! I'm Sundai Johnson Alexander, and this morning we have an exciting announcement that's sure to make waves in our community. We are thrilled to introduce the newest addition to our high school football family, none other than my husband, Bryce Alexander!

Bryce brings with him a wealth of experience, passion, and a love for the game that's contagious. Having coached in various capacities, Bryce has not only honed his skills on the field but has also inspired players to reach their full potential.

As a community, we know the importance of strong leadership, mentorship, and unity in our sports programs, and Bryce is committed to fostering just that. His dedication to not only the game but also to the growth and character development of our young athletes is truly commendable.

So, get ready to witness a new era in New York High School Football. Join me in welcoming Coach Bryce Alexander as he leads our team to victory and instills a sense of pride in our beloved city. Here's to a season filled with passion, teamwork, and the thrill of the game. Go Trojans!

That was the last thing I had to broadcast for the day, so I signed off and waited for the countdown before I moved. I was smiling from ear to ear and proud to announce Bryce's new position, but even more proud to announce our nuptials.

We were married a few months after he popped up in New York. He managed to lower every guard I had in place, but it was for good reason. I rested in the safety of his arms every night. I gave him my heart and he protected it every single day.

The conversation came up as to where we were going to live after we got married, and he didn't hesitate to come to New York, which made me all the happier. I got my man and got to keep my career as well. I knew that my mother was smiling down at both of us.

I walked out of the studio, and he was standing outside waiting for me. He was standing there in a pair of jeans and his high school team's tee shirt. He looked damn good, and I smiled when I saw him.

"Hey, Mrs. Alexander," he said as he pulled me into a kiss.

"Hey, Mr. Alexander," I responded as we broke apart.

"How was your day?" I asked him.

"Great, but it's so much better now,"

"I love you so much, Bryce,"

"I love you, too. Thank you for letting me into your life," he said.

He thanked me, but I felt like I should've been thanking him. He was my person, and his persistence paid off for both of us. I never thought true love existed for me, but I was so happy to be proven wrong. I was blessed and happy, and I was ready to spend the rest of my life making him happy as well.

The End

About the Author

As always, you can keep up with all things Nadia Nicole by emailing me directly at authornadianicole@gmail.com or following me on any or all my social media platforms.

Facebook- www.facebook.com/groups/tpturners

Instagram- www.instagram.com/the_nadia_nicole

Twitter- www.twitter.com/NDaAuthoress

TikTok- www.tiktok.com/@authoress_nadia_nicole

Be sure to join Nadia Nicole's VIP E-Mail list for all exclusives!

Also by Nadia Nicole

Targeted
Bit.ly/buytargeted

Unbothered: The Constance Kelly Story
Bit.ly/GetUnbothered

Pink Panties
Bit.ly/PinkPanties

Free to Be
Bit.ly/FreetoBE

The Quiet Storm Series
The Calm Before the Storm: https://amzn.to/3qV9DDZ

Whirlwind: https://amzn.to/34EQg9g

Aftermath: https://amzn.to/3CB33Xw

Thirst
https://amzn.to/3xsYnBm

The Freestyle Cypher
Bit.ly/FreestyleCypher

Saving Grace
https://amzn.to/47jlpKP

Be sure to check out our other releases:
www.majorkeypublishing.com/novels

To submit a manuscript to be considered, email us at submissions@majorkeypublishing.com

Be sure to LIKE our Major Key Publishing page on Facebook!

Made in the USA
Columbia, SC
05 November 2024

45478616R00091